DEVIL WON'T LET ME BE
A NOVELLA

CHAD FARMER

ALSO AVAILABLE FROM GENREBLAST BOOKS

The Comfy-Cozy Nihilist: A Handbook of Dark Fiction by Nathan D. Ludwig

OTHER WORKS BY CHAD FARMER

"Into This World" (D&T/Godless Emerge Series #13)

Earth Truckers Are Easy (coming August 2023 from D&T Publishing)

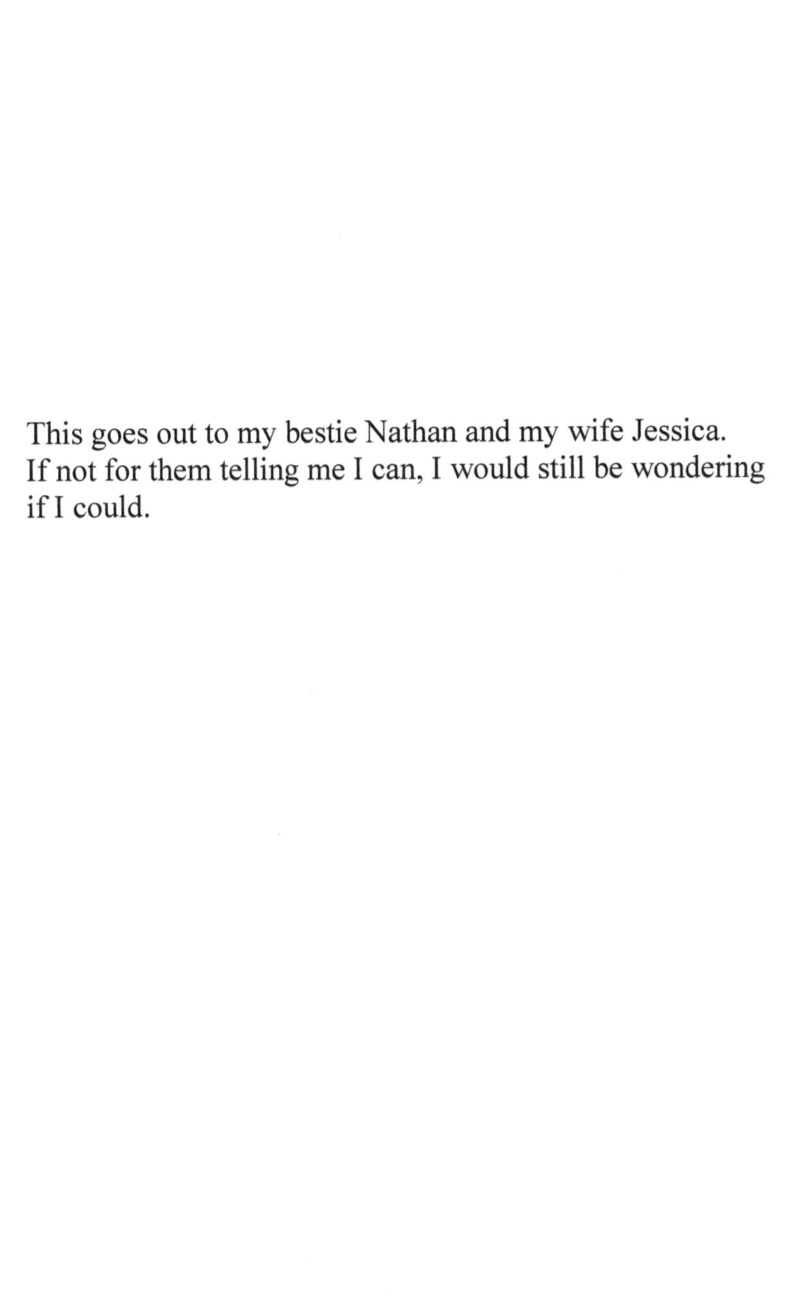

This goes out to my bestie Nathan and my wife Jessica.
If not for them telling me I can, I would still be wondering
if I could.

PROLOGUE

It just so happened that The Devil needed a fresh new way of recruiting souls to the bowels of Hell. To do that, they required someone who was just as cunning and just as evil as themselves. That demonic someone would end up being Ms. Sasha. Lucifer came up with the brilliant idea to send her up to our neck of the woods to do a little wheeling and dealing of the devious and sinister kind. Over the centuries, Lucifer noticed that bullied male teens were an untapped market. Who better to make a deal with these poor unfortunate souls than their seductive temptress provocateur?

As a lowly human of unmemorable origins, Sasha earned her one-way ticket to Hell quite easily. And quite memorably. She was a student at Dimduk College and "dating" Chris Cummingsworth, quarterback for the Dimduk Ducks. A hot, chiseled stud whose cock was beyond legendary. Sasha was, in reality, the team's morale booster; a fluffer for the whole lineup. She was a hit with the boys and was granted access anywhere they went whether it was a home or away game.

As all good things end up though, the college's dean soon put two and two together and ended Sasha's three-hole pre-game pep rallies before those Saturday games. For the past ten years the team had gone 0-12 every season. All of a sudden they were 11-1 just like that. That one loss? Well, Sasha was preoccupied by a urinary tract infection from fiftysomething troglodyte Coach Peter "Petey" Dickers, who used her fuck hole as a urinal after practice one fine day.

The Ducks went on to win the Division III state championship, 56-0. Morale was high. And not as horny as usual. Come to find out the team didn't need Sasha after all once they got going. At least not for every game. After the big win, the boys filed into the locker room, stripped down bare-assed, and entered the shower one by one.

Sasha had rigged all the sprinklers to scalding hot. The shower area filled up with steam. It was sexier that way. Several minutes after the rest of the boys had entered the steam-laden shower room, Chris and his legendary dick strode into the barely visible haze himself.

In her trademark hip-swaying manner, Sasha called out, "Want some hot wet snatch, Cummy Bear?"

Only one person was allowed to call him that.

"You came all the way here just for me, baby?"

Chris's dick sniffed out her pussy like a bloodhound. He plowed her extremely wet and hot meat taco for the next minute or two…or so he thought. After blasting his load, he partially cleared the steam vapors to see their fifteen-year-old mentally challenged equipment boy Allen Deesford lying there dead. And no head. Semen mixed with spinal fluid, blood, and water all spurted out of his neck stump as Chris pulled his dick out of it with a high-pitched scream. Sasha had tricked the poor boy into the showers thinking he would get to hang with the boys like he was a genuine part of the team. He never knew what hit him. To be specific, it was Sasha bludgeoning him with a football helmet until his cranium was crinkly mush. It was easy to remove the kid's head after that.

Sasha eased out of the hot shower vapors, completely naked, and covered in blood. The evil smile she had on her steam-kissed face was just for Chris this time.

Scared shitless, Chris turned and ran but a bar of soap caused him to slip, fall, and crack his dimwitted cranium on the tile. Sasha grabbed a nearby full bottle of shampoo and shoved it right up the barely conscious star jock's wazoonus. Thirteen ounces of dandruff control gel filled up his ass. A jackhammering followed with the rather large plastic bottle until blood shot out of his sphincter and he stopped breathing. Chris never even had a chance to scream over Sasha's uncontrollable laughter.

Chris also never even saw the rest of his team and their fates. Every one of them had had their throats slit from ear to ear with a straight shave razor then subjected to the most foul, unimaginable humiliation and torture any human could endure. With their own toiletries, no less.

All that was left was Coach Dickers, the last one in. He was too fucking dumb to realize none of his primetime, Grade-A athletes had even left the showers yet. He just assumed they were still in there pumping loads of man chowder into whatever skanks they grabbed from the stands along the way. Just another day at the ol' office for his boys.

Once in the shower, he turned off all the shower heads one by one. The steam slowly seeped out and soon enough coach Dickers witnessed the ghastly carnage. There were all his boys sitting against the walls of the shower all in a row with hard dicks never to be fucked again. Blood continued to ooze out of each grinning throat slit and circled the drain. Sasha was crouched over in the corner laughing manically. Covered head-to-toe in blood, piss, shit, and cum. The steam from the water gave her a glistening appearance, beads of water mixed with all of the bodily fluids dripping from her nude sculpture of a body as she stood up and asked the coach with a smile, "Wanna pound my shithole before you turn me in?"

Coach Dickers dropped his pleated grey polyester athletic trousers and pinned Sasha up against the wall and hunched away for all it was worth. He howled out, "Oh-ho you bitch, you're gonna to burn in hell for this!"

"Funny thing about that, Coach. Me and the Devil have already talked!" She moaned, followed by a sinister chuckle.

Just as Dickers was about to empty the swim team into Sasha's colon, the cops busted in and pried the horny old bastard off of Sasha. Before she could say a word, the cops had her hog tied, gagged, and in the squad car. None of this seemed to surprise her, though. She was all smiles all the way.

Sasha pleaded insanity, naturally. For the next ten years, she resided in the Dutra County State Hospital for the Mentally Ill. That all came to an end one rain-soaked afternoon. It was time. She could sense it. Feel it. Their voice was calling her home. An orderly making his rounds delivering lunch found her well after she had bitten off her tongue and bled to death. This was a one-way ticket to Hell. And a swift one at that. Just what she wanted all along.

Truth be known, Sasha had several long conversations with Satan while in the Dutra County State Hospital. Lucifer had been so impressed with her deeds on Earth that they wanted her to head up their new department for dealmaking with bullied teens desperate for payback. Bullied male teens, specifically.

To say she was eager to get to work would be a massive fucking understatement.

This is going to be fun. And easy.

PART ONE
SURVIVING THE EIGHTIES

CHAPTER I

To say Herman and Amanda Masterson had a rough go at life so far would be an outrageous understatement. Herman's left leg was slightly shorter than the right, causing him to wear a platform shoe. If that wasn't embarrassing enough for a kid, you could add a speech impediment to the list due to a partially corrected cleft pallet. The two siblings were abandoned at the ages of five and six; Herman being the youngest. Good ol' Mom and Dad were both professional junkies and hard up for money, so they traded their two bundles of joy for a bundle of crack rock and a couple of demeaning sexual favors to a predictably abusive foster mom.

Until the ages of sixteen and seventeen, Amanda and Herman made the depressing rounds to different foster homes. Each one came with some sort of traumatizing domestic problem. Herman suffered all kinds of abuse; mental and physical. Amanda did not have it much better. Probably worse, even though it's not a competition. Every single foster dad in her life molested her, and one of them even got her pregnant as a bonus. After only a couple of seconds of Amanda hearing her baby girl's premature heartbeat, it was snatched from her young mother arms and adopted posthaste.

The torment seemingly ended when Amanda discovered that they had an uncle by marriage who lived about a few hours away in Dutra County. She was beaten for an hour straight with a metal colander after using the computer in their latest foster dad's office to find that out. Will Jameson was a meager and unassuming school security guard at Dutra High School. Just promoted to head of security at the school according to the local news report.

The two wayward orphans were ecstatic to find out that their horrible lives of torment, sexual abuse, and constant ridicule were about to end for good. After skipping school to meet them secretly at the mall for a nervous lunch of food court Chinese, Will lawyered up and the rest was, as they say, history. It was just in time for summer break when they moved in with their savior uncle. One thing Will failed to do was mention the sordid history of the Dutra family, who owned Dutra County lock, stock, and barrel. Including their next stop: Ezekiel Dutra High School. It was a lot to absorb, so he figured he'd wait until they had settled in and were ready for their first semester to give them a heads up.

Though their uncle hadn't been the head of security for too long at Dutra High. He'd loudly vowed to clean the place of "lower learning" and return it to the respectable beacon of education that it once was long ago. Little did he know before the big promotion, it was going to take a lot more than monitoring the halls for truant teenagers or busting adolescents smoking in the bathrooms to make a difference.

The big day had arrived; the first day of school for Herman and Amanda. Tenth grade for Herman and eleventh for Amanda. Both were optimistic but still a bit gun shy. Herman sat in his room psyching himself up with a worn, rubber werewolf mask on. He had been fascinated with the fantastical creatures ever since he was a pup. A werewolf had no fear, its strength was unmatched, and with the moon on their side, one could rip the asshole out of a grizzly bear without blinking an eye. His room was wallpapered with every movie poster that had a werewolf within. Silver Bullet, American Werewolf in London, The Howling, Late Phases, you name it. But it was Dog Soldiers that was his all-time favorite. Bad Moon was a close second. He always got a kick out of scaring Amanda with his mask. It gave him a sense of power knowing he was feared by at least one human being in this world. Even if for just a little bit.

As bad as life had dragged Amanda through the ringer, she was still full of life and optimism. And a healthy sense of humor. After fighting off lecherous pedophile foster dads, Amanda wasn't scared of anyone anymore. She felt free and unafraid in her uncle's house. In her mind, her bravery was just courage under fire in the worst circumstances. Spitting in the face of the devil. The physical and mental abuse endured by Herman didn't make him any stronger, however. In fact, right the opposite happened. The meek, mild, and scared-of-a-fly teen developed a proverbial tortoise shell. Any sign of danger and Herman would retreat. Amanda, on the other hand, would grit her teeth, dig the heels in, and fight like a honey badger. It made the beatings worse, but she regretted nothing.

To try to build Herman's self-confidence, Amanda would always act frightened when he would sneak into her bedroom. She didn't want to hurt his feelings. This morning he was sure to give her the scare of her life. Not only did he have his werewolf mask on, but he also bought a pair of fake fangs at the seasonal Spookarama Halloween store. It was one of those costume chains that would rent out an abandoned building for two months then disappear as soon the season was over.

Herman crept slowly down the hall; his best werewolf stance activated. Uncle Will had already left for work. Amanda was in her room, sitting on her bed wearing nothing but a pair of panties and a modest b-cup bra. She gently brushed her shoulder-length sandy blonde hair. She was the type that knew damn well she was beautiful but pretended to be oblivious. It made her existence a little easier up until then.

Herman cracked the door open to her bedroom and stood there in awe at the innocent beauty of his sister. It wasn't incest or anything weird like that. Herman just looked up to his sister. She was the only one that ever cared for or looked after him. He often wondered why he couldn't be braver like his fearless sister. She was a beautiful angel of mercy and strength in his eyes.

He opened the door further, limped in, and sat next to her on her bed. With his inescapable lisp he asked his sister, "You think thith year ith going to be better? I'm really kinda thcared."

"Just be confident and don't take shit from anyone," she said with a wink.

Herman lowered his shoulders and bowed his head sheepishly. "Eathy for you to thay, thith. But I'll try."

Amanda stood up, glided to her closet, and selected a simple but stylish yellow sundress with spaghetti straps and slipped it over her pale, lithe body. She turned, looked at Herman, and with a smile said, "Sit up and keep that back straight, Hermy."

Herman took his mask off, and Amanda gave him a slight peck on the cheek. The bulk of Herman's optimism had been left behind a long time ago in the sock he would shove up his ass so his foster dads couldn't shove their dick up there. They just ended up dry humping his ass crack, because why stop when you're hard as fuck? Being five-foot-four and weighing no more than a hundred and thirty pounds sopping wet caused the poor weakling to be a constant target for pedophile foster dads, a stiff breeze, and most (if not all) bullies. So he needed a confidence whenever he could get it.

Amanda finished getting ready while Herman hustled down to the kitchen and devoured a fried egg sandwich (extra mayo) and some breakfast sausage left on the table by Uncle Will. Amanda made her way into the kitchen and found a banana and a bagel for herself. Her breakfasts were never much because she was always watching her figure. At least that's what she always told Herman. Soon, the two were ready to start their first day at school. As they were leaving, Uncle Will called Amanda. Herman was already outside by the car waiting on his sister. The car Will gifted them when they moved in. It was a shocking surprise on top of their hard-won new freedom. Amanda fainted when she saw it. It wasn't anything special, just an old four-door grocery getter, but it was the thought and the effort that floored her.

Amanda answered her phone with the usual, "Wassup, Unc?"

Uncle Will's voice seemed filled with concern. "Overheard you and your brother talking about the homecoming party this weekend at the No Tell Motel east of the railroad tracks. I'm asking you nicely not to go. That place is a cesspool of drugs, sex, pimps, junkies, and hookers. Also, that's where that Debbie Dutra hangs out and you do not want to cross paths with her inside or outside of school, okay?"

"Well, the drugs and sex part don't seem so bad. Two out of five is solid, right?"

"That's not funny. You wanna tell that one to your therapist?"

"Okay Unc, I got it. We won't go, I promise. But how will I make any friends? Those kinda things are where high school kids really bond, you know?"

Will chuckled over the phone. "Sweetheart there's no doubt in my mind that you'll make friends. You got a great personality and most of all, you're extremely attractive; just like me."

Amanda rolled her eyes and grinned. "If you say so Unc, have a good day, luv yah!" Amanda hung up and ran outside to meet up with Herman.

Off to the first day of school in their new lives.
Off to see the rest of their lives take shape.

12

CHAPTER II

Amanda and Herman pulled into the parking lot of Ezekiel Dutra High School. Named after the founder of Dutra County, E.F. Dutra. Way back in 1832. Ancient stuff. Poison to high schoolers.

It was a sweaty nutsack of the worst kind. The rectangular stone sign outside read:

DUTRA HIGH SCHOOL - LEARNING WITH INTEGRITY.

Etched there long ago, no doubt since that was an inaccurate statement nowadays. The place was overrun with illegal drugs and prostitution. Sexual harassment and assault were a daily occurrence with both students and faculty. The currently residing principal, Dr. Farley Lipshitz, took an extra special interest in young girls, though he wouldn't turn down a fat boy's asshole in a pinch. There were metal detectors at each entrance but those were no longer functioning due to being vandalized, dismantled, and chopped up for parts at the hands of some unruly teens. Several times. So they just gave up installing new ones. Graffiti warned of violence of all kinds and threatened various members of the faculty and local government. Quite charming overall.

Amanda parked their sputtering grocery getter in the nearest empty spot she saw. She didn't even think to consider why that spot was still empty in a sea of filled spots.

It was, in fact, Debbie Dutra's parking spot.

Deborah Demarest Dutra; the daughter of the one-and-only Sheriff Raymond Dutra. The source of all corruption and iniquity in Dutra County. The latest despot in a long line of demented, psychopathic Dutra descendants.

There were very few good and decent students that attended Dutra High. Those unfortunates were harassed, bullied, and extorted for their lunch money daily by a high school gang called "The Eighties." There were only three members; Debbie Dutra, Grant "Shades" McGuffin, and Fuck Yeah. And there only needed to be three members, as all of them had a list of offenses longer than the gen pop of a major state jail. All three dressed in authentic 1980s high school clothes and mostly spoke in Eighties slang. To say they were feared amongst the teachers and students alike would be like saying lots of water is made up of little drops of water.

Shades always wore some jackassedy 80s world tour rock-n-roll band t-shirt that was way too tight (today it was Winger), acid wash jeans, and a pair of white Reebok high tops with Velcro straps. He almost never took his sunglasses off. And when he did, it was most likely to better sexually assault someone. Fuck Yeah's freight elevator didn't quite reach the top floor. Just kinda idled there loudly. No one knew why and were afraid to ask. He was about six-foot-five, topped the scale at well over three hundred pounds, wore his dad's letterman jacket with the sleeves torn off, and sported a mullet that was the envy of any hard rock or country star from four decades ago. The towering oaf had the strength of a gorilla and the I.Q. of a pet rock. He could only say "Oh fuck yeah, fuck yeah…" no matter what the situation or conversation called for. Debbie and Shades could figure out what he was saying, and they even developed their own dialect for him, dubbed "Fuckyesish" but to anyone else it was Greek and Latin combined.

The raddest and baddest muscle machine at Dutra High belonged to none other than Shades and it was closing in on Debbie's newly occupied parking spot. It was an '83 V-8 candy apple red Trans Am with T-tops. It was a mean motor scooter to the most radical extreme. Debbie always rode shotgun. Fuck Yeah was content to fill up the back seat with his gigantic frame. It didn't take even two seconds for Debbie to realize new kids were in their parking spot. No one with half a brain would dare park there that went there regularly. The Eighties pulled up right behind Amanda and Herman. "Let's Get Physical" from Olivia Newton John blasted through the speakers of Shades' disco night club-on-wheels.

Shades slid out of his car, walked around the back, opened the passenger side door, and made the following announcement as Debbie remained in the seat. It was mandatory any time a new student needed to know who Debbie was.

"Do not stare directly into the sunlight, but acknowledge the presence of the baddest, most awesomest fuck machine on high heels. She makes young boys cream their jeans and turns all the girls into righteous lesbos. She's everything Pat Benatar, Madonna, and Joan Jett thought they were. Here she is, Ms. Debbie Dutra!"

A pair of hot pink, open-toed high heeled shoes with a strap wrapped around just above the ankle appeared first. Shades extended his right hand to assist Debbie to the curb. Some nearby pencil-necked geek violently convulsed and made a big wet spot in his khakis after noticing the camel toe Debbie was more than willing to show off behind her skintight fire engine red leotards. Two erect nipples peaked through a tissue paper-thin, tight-laced sports bra. Shades flicked the most erect one, then bent down and licked it. Debbie closed her eyes in euphoric ecstasy and moaned, "Make sure that new bitch knows my name." She pointed to where Amanda and Herman were with a shiny, candy apple green fingernail.

Shades strutted over confidently, and gently tapped several times on Amanda's window.

"Ith thith the kidth Unc warned uth about?" Herman asked as he cowered in the backseat.

"Probably. That didn't take long at all," Amanda said, gripping the steering wheel in annoyance.

"What do we do?"

"Where do we come from?"

"…you know."

"Where do we come from, Herman?"

"We came from Hell to be here."

"…and?"

"…and if we came from Hell, how bad can thith place be."

"Right. Do you believe it?"

"Yeth. Yeah, I believe it." Herman flashed her a weak smile.

Shades' window tapping only got more insistent.

"Helloooo? Anyone in that shitbox? You are illegally parked, dumbfucks!"

Amanda rolled the window down about halfway and asked, "Yes? Can I help you?"

Shades pulled his sunglasses just below his eyes, squatted down to the level of her window, and asked her with a crooked smile, "You ever order a hotdog at a drive thru?"

Herman looked over at the dreadful scowl on Debbie's face. The hairs on the back of Herman's neck stood up as Shades spoke in his annoying deep, nasally tone.

"No, I don't like hot dogs too much," Amanda deadpanned.

Shades stood back up, unzipped his pants, took out his dick, and placed it right in front of Amanda's face. After fluffing it a few times, the erect penis bounced up and down like a diving board as Shades thumped it against the window. A speckle of clear precum dribbled out and landed on Amanda's lap.

Disgusted but not shocked, Amanda rolled up her window extra fast. Shades screamed at the top of his lungs like a whiny little schoolgirl as his love muscle swelled up and turned three shades of blue. "You goddamn bitch, roll the window down now, or I'm gonna skull fuck your eye sockets!"

Amanda and Herman laughed hysterically as Shades pounded on the roof of Amanda's car bellowing in pain. Tears rolled down his cheeks. But at the same time, Shade's meat pistol shot out pudding bullets like a missile, passed Amanda's face, ricocheted off Herman's left cheek and landed on the inside of the window shield. The creamy human donut glaze trickled down the window slowly. From the outside Shades yelled out, "The bitch made me cum!"

Debbie heard Shades screaming out in pain and forced ecstasy and frowned.

"No pussy for you tonight unless you get back in this car right now!"

There was Shades, pleading for his dick's very existence, when the oversized bag of whale shit known as Dewey Wilcox came wobbling up. Always appearing when things couldn't get any more fucked. He made Fuck Yeah look svelte. Redundant waves of cellulite roiled within and without his always-too-small garments. His greasy hair partially covered a face riddled with whiteheads and pus-oozing zits. He wore a fake "I Love the 80s" Wal-Mart t-shirt that pushed hard against sizable man tits and his underarms wreaked of fatty food-inspired body odor. It was Dewey's dream to be in The Eighties. His every waking thought consisted of this goal. The sight of him repulsed Debbie (audibly) but being an opportunist, she would use him frequently to bully more kids than she could handle on her own.

Not realizing (or caring) that Shades' dick was impossibly jammed in between the window and door frame, Dewey grabbed him around the waist from behind and began to pull. Hard. Shades grimaced in pain as his dick stretched out like a hairy rubber band. On the inside of the car, the tip of his cock was well past turning beet red and turning dark purple. And it was now crying little drips of blood. Shades called out again "Quit pulling lard ass, you're gonna rip it in half!"

Amanda rolled down her window with a sudden jerk, releasing Shades from her car's grasp, and rolled it back up just as fast. Shades limped back to his car with a swollen, stretched out, two-inches-too-long dick and his damaged male ego, yelling to Debbie, "That whore jammed my dick up! She's gotta pay for that!"

Dewey attempted to console Shades with a hearty "Nobody fucks with the Eighties!"

The veins on Shades' cock throbbed relentlessly as he rolled it up like a belt and tucked the bruised boy behind his zebra print Jockey underwear. He eased back into the driver's seat like molasses and pouted as quietly as he could with a bright red face. The color of ultimate humiliation.

"You happy now? Did you meet the new kids? Everything copasetic, shithead?"

"Yes," Shades whined like a kicked puppy.

Dewey wobbled his fat ass over to the Trans Am and asked Debbie "Was a good thing I was there to help Shades, right Deb? Say, ya want me to, you know, take care of 'em boss lady?" Beads of fatty sweat dripped into the interior of Shades' car.

"I don't care what the fuck you do! Just make sure they know who The Eighties are and what we're all about!"

Back in their own car, Amanda turned to Herman with a look of determination. He was about to put his werewolf mask on, scared shitless at the aggression on display.

"Don't put that on. Everything's going to be fine, okay? I'm gonna go say something."

"Manda, no. Don't. It'th our firtht day. You're thuppothed to lay low on the firtht day. Thith ith the exact oppothite of laying low."

"And hide behind a werewolf mask? Life isn't about escaping, Hermy. It's right here in front of us. You have to confront it head on. For better or for worse. You dig?"

Her look of anger softened to a smile just for Herman. Herman nodded slightly, reaching to take off his mask. Amanda didn't wait for him to respond, she popped out of the car and took a few angry steps over to Shades' Trans Am.

"Hey!"

Her shout was directed at Debbie, who seemed confused.

"I think she's talking to you, boss," Dewey warbled at her.

"...The Fuck?" Debbie craned her head to her left to see who was up in their business.

The fucking new bitch.

"I said, hey you, slut!"

"Oh, shit, she's definitely talking to you," Shades half-chuckled.

Debbie slapped him on the back of the head. "Shut the fuck up."

Amanda was right up on the passenger side door, leaving just enough room for it to open.

"Get out of the car, skank!"

"I know you did not just—" Debbie uttered as she got out, all in a huff. Before she could finish, Amanda kicked her right in her muff. The point of her toe slightly entered inside her vaginal territory. Debbie fell back in her seat, grabbing her crotch with both hands.

"Ah, that fucking hurt you stupid new bitch. Dewey! Shades! Fuck yeah! Kill this bitch!"

Inside their car, Herman had put his werewolf mask back on and was now cowering on the floor of the backseat in abject terror. No help for Amanda there. But she didn't need any. She was ready to take on the whole gang right then and there.

Shades limped back out of his car and let the backseat down for Fuck Yeah to get out and unfurl his massive frame. They're joined by Dewey as they converge on Amanda.

"You fucked with the wrong girl, new bitch." Debbie groaned from the passenger seat.

Just as the three guys were on top of a scowling, balled up-fisticuffs-brandishing Amanda, an older, steadier voice pierced the tension.

"There a problem here?" Uncle Will was making his rounds and spotted the commotion as he came around the building in his golf cart. His means of transportation may have been goofy, but his means of protection wasn't. He carried a Smith & Wesson .38 revolver on his hip. His hand was currently on the handle, steady and still.

"Debbie Dutra. Of course it's you. I'm kinda sorta getting tired of seeing you around."

The Eighties and Dewey eyed Will caressing his revolver and backed off Amanda. Debbie slammed her car door and sat back, folding her arms like a toddler.

"Get in the fucking car. I need ice for my pussy."

"I'll get it!" Dewey shouts over to her.

Fuck Yeah, highly amused at all of this, sat back down in his seat, just chuckling. "Oh fuck yeah, fuck yeah…" As Shades got back in, Fuck Yeah pointed at Shades' crotch with excited jazz hands. "Fuck yeah!" Then pointed at Debbie's crotch. More chuckling from him. "Fuuuuuck Yeahhhh!"

Debbie reached back and popped him on the mouth. "Shut the hell up and lick the window, retard." Fuck Yeah smashed his head into the window and licked it gladly.

Debbie addressed both of her now well-behaved hounds in a much calmer manner. "We will deal with them all later." The Trans Am peeled off down the aisle of parked cars and eventually found a parking space.

Will looked over to Amanda now that The Eighties were out of sight. He nodded solemnly at her.

"You okay?"

She returned his nod begrudgingly.

"Are you going to be there every time we need saving?" She asked with a frown.

"I'm gonna try."

Amanda let out a smirk at that and gave him a half-hearted thumbs up.

"Where's your brother?"

She jerked her head toward their car with a grimace.

"Probably peeing his pants. Don't blame him, though."

"We gotta toughen that kid up. Sounds like a job for big sis."

"And big uncle, too."

"We'll see. Get to class, okay?"

"Thanks, Unc."

Amanda returned to their car, adrenaline slowly subsiding in her. The reality of what they had just experienced started to set in as Herman reappeared from the back seat and slid his werewolf mask off; the danger gone for now.

"You kicked that girl in the faginah."

"Vagina. And yes, I did."

"She was mean as heck."

"Yes, she was. But a lot of bullies are loud until you-"

"Kick 'em in the vah-gy-nah."

Amanda laughed and tussled Herman's hair.

"That'll take care of them for now. Between my foot and Unc's gun, we'll get by. We've been through worse, right?"

"Yeah, we've been through Hell."

"That's right."

CHAPTER III

Dewey was waiting for Herman and Amanda just past the threshold to the school's entrance. Herman quickly and involuntarily met one of the front doors with his face. The force from it knocked him clear off his feet and sent him to the floor. Amanda tried to help her brother up, but Dewey grabbed her and pinned her against a nearby locker and gave her the lowdown with his shit-smelling breath.

"Listen little miss new bitch; nobody fucks with The Eighties. You better grow eyes in the back of your pretty little head because payback is an ugly, ugly bitch, you got tha—"

A maintenance closet door opened abruptly next to them, and elderly school janitor Johnny Dimwether shuffled out. Everyone just called him Janitor Johnny, though. He sported a salt-and-pepper handlebar mustache and a beard that hung just below the chin. His sudden appearance combined with his deep baritone voice stopped Dewey in his tracks as it echoed through the halls.

"Dewey Wilcox, your presence is unwanted. I would advise you to cease in your evil deeds and report to your assigned classroom. Now!"

Dewey backed up cautiously from Amanda, his foul body sweat drenching the front of Amanda's sun dress. The outline of her bra seeped through the cotton fabric. Johnny slowly approached Dewey, who was in a state of shock. Soon he was face-to-face with the frozen wannabe Eighties lackey. Johnny stared into the eyes of Dewey for what seemed like an eternity. Dewey let out a loud, wet fart when the stoned-faced janitor blinked unexpectedly. The smell of runny shit drifted up to the nostrils of all involved.

Dewey held his hands over his ass and retreated to the boy's bathroom.

Amanda smiled with surprise and amusement at the mysterious janitor while she helped Herman to his feet.

"Thank you kind sir, what's your name?" As Amanda turned around, Johnny was gone.

"That was weird. Oh well, guess we better get to class. That's what we are here for, right? Forgot in all this commotion," Amanda said as she playfully elbowed her bewildered brother. Herman agreed with a shaky nod. Both parted ways and ventured to their assigned classrooms.

"And no werewolf mask!" Amanda called out after him.

"Okay, thith, but no promitheth," he answered sheepishly.

*****

Debbie Dutra stomped into her homeroom. Late, as usual. All the boys were usually ogling at her as she passed by them to get to her seat way in the back. Even Chet Brockman, Debbie's go-to meathead fuckstick when she was burnt out on Shades' dick. And seeing as Shades' baloney pony was going to be out of order for a bit, Chet would absolutely have to do.

Chet Brockman was the high school quarterback. By default. Debbie threatened to sodomize anyone else who tried out for the position. She always made him wear his football helmet and shoulder pads. Everywhere. To class. In the shower. During sex. It made her wetter than an otter snorkeling under a waterfall. He was the typical jock with his fabricated weight room muscles, acid wash blue jeans that were tucked into his cowboy boots, and a t-shirt that read PROPERTY OF DEBBIE DUTRA! STAY AWAY SKANKS!

Mrs. Langford, the fit and trim fortysomething teacher in charge of this homeroom immediately caught the category five hurricane that was brewing in Debbie's eyes. Unlike most teachers at Dutra High, Mrs. Langford wasn't intimidated by Debbie or her goon squad. She was new. New-ish.

It was unwritten law at Dutra High that no boys were supposed to be attracted to any other girl other than Debbie Dutra. But it was also a fact that Chet Brockman wasn't the sharpest spoon in the drawer. This was verified yet again when Debbie caught the dimwitted jock passing a note to Amanda. Debbie intercepted the crumpled-up piece of paper before it could reach the new bitch. Inside were the scribblings equivalent to an eight-year-old boy. And that was being kind. It read, "want too fuk?" Under it were two boxes and the words, "chek yes or now."

Mrs. Langford snatched the note from Debbie's hand, read it, and put her hands on her hips as she glared at Ms. Dutra.

"Report to the principal's office right now."

Amanda tried to cover up her smile at the sight of Debbie being embarrassed in front of everyone, but it was too late. Debbie snatched a handful of Amanda's hair and pulled hard, trying to yank it out of her head. Debbie whispered into Amanda's ear, "Listen here, new bitch. This isn't over. You already had it coming but now it's gonna be even worse. Buckle the fuck up." She let go of Amanda's clump of hair with a violent jerk of her hand.

"We're not scared of you, skank. I've seen a dozen lowlifes just like you. Deep down you're just another loudmouth coward."

"Oh yeah? You better watch your goddamn back." Debbie blew a kiss at Amanda and stomped out of the door on her high heels like they were cloven hooves.

Mrs. Langford followed her out the door, yelling "That's it, Ms. Dutra, I'm going to make sure you're expelled!

"Are you okay, Ms. Masterson?" Mrs. Langford asked Amanda, turning back to the snickering classroom.

"I'll live," Amanda said with a grimace as she rubbed her head.

*****

As Debbie stormed down the hall, she noticed Janitor Johnny staring at her as he mopped the floors. With one kick, she knocked the mop bucket over and yelled, "What's your fucking major malfunction, you jive turkey?!" Johnny just smiled and continued to mop up the floor as if he was deaf.

Or as if he knew something she didn't.

CHAPTER IV

Inside the oppressive stink of the principal's tiny office prison, Debbie pulled her t-shirt down to expose just a little more cleavage, hoping to seduce the principal into submission. Not that it was hard. The principal of Dutra High was a degenerate candy snatching scumbag who went by the name of Dr. Farley Lipshitz. He had a degree in child psychology, which was convenient as he was an avid fan of them in more ways than one. His main interest was to see how many pictures he could take of teenage girls' asses during the school day with his tired-ass flip phone. He spent most of the day jerking off to downloaded videos of schoolgirls undressing in the cheerleader's locker room. There was a hidden button cam behind one of the air vents that he installed himself. Even his physical presence was oppressive with a bad oily comb over, asymmetrical beer gut, and noticeable dandruff on each shoulder of his blazer. And lemonade yellow-stained teeth.

To gain entry into Lipshitz's dank lair, Debbie had to strut by his secretary, Mrs. Madison. An elderly but sharp-as-a-tack employee of the Dutra County Public School System. She refused to greet Debbie as she looked down at her through elegant but conservative brown plastic-rimmed bifocals. She had nothing but dreadful contempt for Deborah, but she was about two years shy of retirement and it couldn't get here soon enough. It kept her from voicing her opinion of Ms. Dutra out loud. Her glares and stares were enough. She was greeted today by a middle finger and a trademark disrespectful greeting from Debbie, "Eat shit and die bitch."

Mrs. Madison matched the gesture with a little taunt. "Let me guess, Mrs. Langford made you write on the chalkboard one hundred times how bad you've been before coming in here."

Debbie thought better of trading barbs with the old bat. There was much more urgent business to attend to. That desk-riding fossil would get hers one day soon. She blustered past the reception area and stormed into Lipshitz's inner sanctum.

"I've heard you have been a very bad girl. Is this true, Ms. Dutra?"

Debbie smiled wide as she pulled her shirt down a little more so he could drool over her wares. Then she gently raised her pointer finger to her mouth, bit on it ever so gently while looking at Lipshitz with fake innocence and cooed, "And if I was?" She rose, circled her way around to the principal's chair, wheeled his fat ass out from behind the desk, and unzipped his pants to reveal a shriveled-up little thimble of a cock with patchwork grey pubes and dried chunks of semen encrusted here and there. Debbie tried not to laugh involuntarily.

"You going to make me wet with that academic jackhammer, or what?"

The principal sniffed the air like a diabetic bloodhound, smiled a toothy grin, and began jerking off with his thumb and pointer finger in a tight O shape. He didn't need any lube because his smegma-encased weenis provided enough grease to reduce the friction.

"Are you going to douche after this?" His tongue was now hanging out the side of his mouth as his finger O moved back and forth in rapid succession.

"Probably not. Is that a problem?" Debbie removed the principal's hand to pleasure him with hers. The smell of spoiled sardines and an unclean tube steak didn't seem to bother Debbie one iota. Business was business. If she was going to keep the drugs flowing (and by extension the cash) she had to woman up and service the faculty in all kinds of proactive ways.

"The nastier the better." The principal moaned while his tongue hung out like a thirsty and panting dog.

While she was in there, she might as well go in for the kill, as it were.

"What are you going to do about that bitch teacher Mrs. Langford always insulting me and thinking she's better than me?"

"Wh-hat exactll-y has she done?" He asked her as thick webs of drool dribbled from the corner of his mouth.

Debbie stopped for a second, wiped his mouth with her finger and uses the drool in her hand to help jerk him to completion.

"Remember the class lecture on how mad she was that the school was named after the Dutras and the lies Mrs. she told about my great great granddaddy? Hm?"

Debbie stopped tugging away to remind the principal of the history of the Dutras and their influence in the town. A topic she was a bona fide scholar in from a very young age.

Lipshitz went limp and sagged into his chair.

"I think your ancestors have more than gotten their revenge. Dutras have bullied their way into every position of power in this town."

"Come again?"

"Earned their way into every position of power, I meant to say."

"That's what I figured you said."

"Are you gonna finish me off or do I have to assign some detention your way, Ms. Dutra?"

"Point is, a Dutra never forgets, and we always win in the end. That's where the school got its name you cock-diseased, dandruff-flaked pervert!"

"Okay, okay what do you want me to do?"

"Fire her, I'll take care of the rest."

Lipshitz looked down at his slowly rising slime-and-saliva-drenched pecker.

"Sure. Now hop to, eh?"

"Don't fuck with me, fatty! Either can her ass or I'll make a phone call to Mrs. Lipshitz and tell her about her blobfuck husband and his unusual and aggressive fondness for young girls and barely hairy muffs."

The principal jumped up with pants and underwear around his ankles in a clumsy panic.

"You… You just wait a hot ass minute Missy! I run this school. Nobody threatens me, understand?"

Debbie grabbed the desk phone to dial the Lipshitz residence.

The principal pressed the hang up button on his phone, bowed his head in shame and mumbled, "I, uh… I guess I will be firing uh, Mrs. Langford, effective immediately."

Satisfied with the moment, Debbie grabbed ahold of Lipshitz's thumbdick and finished him off in less than sixty seconds. He blew his chunky yellow load into a nearby trashcan that already had several crusty tissue papers.

"One of these days I'm going to be clearheaded when you stomp in here and I'll expel you once and for all."

"Uh uh, my daddy will hang you by your tiny little schlong before you get a chance to do shit. Remember who owns this fucking town." Debbie smacked her own ass and pranced out of the office.

On her way out, Debbie spotted Janitor Johnny walking into an unmarked door further down the main hallway. She followed him out of sheer boredom. And the hopes of further harassment. Debbie reached the door and opened it but all she saw was a room filled with old broken-down desks, cobwebs, and textbooks that dated back to the 1950s. A black widow spun its web above her as she yelled out after the old janitor in anger and confusion.

"Where'd you go, you ole pervert?!"

There was nowhere for him to go once inside that old-ass room. Eventually Debbie gave up looking at the past and slammed the door shut with a tight little frown.

CHAPTER V

The school day had ended with certainty and the halls were littered with notebook paper, candy wrappers, and spilled soda drinks. And drugs. For some odd reason, Johnny always seemed to clean it up with ease all by himself. It was as if he had some mystical powers that were overqualified for cleaning boogers off bathroom walls, gum underneath seats, and other sordid things.

Amanda and Herman decided to hang back, way back, hoping Debbie and her henchmen would be completely out of sight. Amanda had texted Uncle Will and made up a story about staying after late for study hall. On the first day. She cringed at her lie. She received a thumbs up as a response. The fib was good enough, apparently. Herman refused to leave the school until it was absolutely safe, and Amanda wasn't going to leave him alone like this. It was hardwired in her DNA to look out for her weirdo brother no matter what.

The sun had gone down at least an hour ago and it was virtually pitch black. Amanda and Herman had waited long enough. Both decided the coast was as clear as it was going to be. Herman hoped they could cut through the athletic wing, then across the football field behind the school and make it to the parking lot undetected. With football practice over, all the jocks, coaches, and cheerleaders had left everything nice and empty. The only light was a nearby bug zapper frying insects one after another. Herman worried his fate would be the same unless he could make it to their car safely. He darted across the field against his sister's half-whispered warnings. She wanted to take the long way around, but Herman insisted a sprint across the field would make things easier. Halfway to the other side a now familiar voice called out from the bleachers "Blue 42, Blue 42, hut, hut!" The stadium lights flickered on, temporarily blinding Herman. Fuck Yeah was running at him full speed in his full football regalia - helmet, jersey, pads, spiked cleats. The works.

Amanda tried to warn Herman, but it was too late. Fuck Yeah blindsided Herman full force as Amanda shrieked automatically. The All-State nose tackle connected so hard that he knocked the wind out of Herman's frail body and rendered him unconscious. Amanda rushed out onto the field to check on him, ignoring any further danger that might have lurked in the shadows. Fuck Yeah kept running after the vicious attack, ending up in the end zone. The unintelligible whacko performed some worn out celebratory dance as if he'd just won the Super Bowl. He yelled at the top of his lungs "Oh fuck yeah, fuck yeah…!" while Amanda attempted desperately to revive her brother.

"Herman, please! We gotta get out of here. Wake up!"

The familiar voice belonged to the dementedly delighted Debbie Dutra, stationed up in the darkened bleachers. She was dressed in a cheerleader's outfit that was two sizes too small. At least. Sitting next to her, sucking on her neck meat and giving her a good finger fucking was Shades. His two middle fingers were jackhammering away inside Debbie's foul entryway. For the moment, Debbie squirted in response to the fingering like a malfunctioning water fountain. No moans of pleasure though, this was business as usual for her. And for Shades too. A puddle of she-cum drenched the metal bench where they were perched.

The sadistic duo soon descended from the bleachers after Debbie had caused a flood in section B, row 15. Shades cheered Fuck Yeah on for the radically awesome tackle.

"Gnarly sack, my dude! I think you left him alive, though."

Fuck Yeah foamed at the mouth and ran back to the fifty-yard line where Amanda was attempting to wake up her brother. She gave Herman a hard smack and he stirred briefly, letting out a weak groan.

Debbie clapped while taunting Amanda, who was shaking Herman violently. "I told you to watch your back, new bitch."

Amanda felt in her soul what was coming and she just cracked, past all of her forced bravado and years of discipline in the face of relentless abuse. She knew instinctively that this right here was coming from a place of pure sadism and malice without an ounce of guilt or self-loathing, unlike all those pathetic foster parents. She let out a slight sob, both her body and her mind betraying her wishes all at once.

"Look, Debbie, I was just defending my brother. He doesn't deserve whatever you're—"

Shades was on her before she could finish and backhanded Amanda, sending her face right into the damp, post-evening sprinkler sod.

"Fuck yo face bitch! I can't even jerk it to Debbie. Had to finger blast her because of you! And fuck your window, too!"

Debbie slipped her damp, ripe-smelling panties off and placed them gently over Amanda's face.

"You know what's the bee's knees after a getting the ol' hip lip serviced?" She asked Amanda.

Debbie then straddled, squatted, and sat on Amanda's chest. Piss streamed out of her and saturated Debbie's already period-stained panties. Amanda coughed and gagged for air as urine seeped into her mouth.

Shades looked severely discontented.

"I thought you were going to save the golden shower for me?"

"It's called waterboarding, you dumb fuck."

Nearby, Fuck Yeah laughed oafishly as Debbie smeared her muff in Amanda's face to dry off and dismounted with a smack to her damp face.

"Fuck Yeah, come here. I got a secret to tell you, baby."

Fuck Yeah plodded over, took off his helmet, bent down and listened with a stupid grin. No sooner than she could finish her secret, Fuck Yeah undressed in less than a minute flat. There he stood in all his glory with a jock strap that was on backwards and a hard cock that was at least a baker's dozen of inches.

Debbie grasped Fuck Yeah's dick and guided him towards Amanda. The girth of Fuck Yeah's mule-sized warhammer caused a guttural, ear-deafening scream from Amanda. Shades paced back and forth in anticipation all the while. Debbie noticed his angst.

"A hole is a hole right?"

Shades was on the exact same wavelength as Debbie. He glanced over at Herman, barely moving. The stadium lights were by now near full illumination. Shade strode over to Herman with utter boldness, loosened his belt, pulled down his jeans and underwear, and within the same motion, yanked off Herman's sweatpants and tighty whiteys, and jammed his pointer finger into Herman's shitter to check for tightness.

"A lot firmer than that freshman I finagled my dick into last Christmas. What was his name? Roberto? Can never remember that shit." Shades spat on each hand, rubbed them together, coated his dick and impaled his swollen rod deep into Herman for all it was worth.

Herman was coming out of his Fuck Yeah-induced stupor to the point of being able to recognize things visually just in time to notice Amanda on her back with Debbie straddled over her and Fuck Yeah standing over them with the biggest erection he'd ever seen. And then the sensation of being anally violated repeatedly took over everything else. As he squealed in pain, he reached out in vain for his sister in hopes that would get her to move but she looked beyond terrified and didn't make eye contact with Herman once. He was quickly met with a tight fist grasping his hair and smashing his face into the ground with brutal force. Several teeth and blood spewed from his mouth. Herman returned to la-la land just as quick as he came out of it.

Shades yelled out gleefully as he continued to pound Herman's ass, "Spiked the football! Touchdown!"

Fuck Yeah congratulated him, stroking his monster dick violently.

"Oh Fuck Yeah, fuck yeah…!"

Debbie was running out of patience, sucking on her teeth and snapping her fingers at her men.

"Get your dumb ass down there and teach that bitch a lesson with your tard trunk!"

Fuck Yeah wiped slobber from his mouth while inching closer and closer to Amanda. The only way to know she was still alive were shallow breaths from a barely rising chest. The gargantuan of The Eighties punched Amanda in the stomach when she realized he was about to enter her and forced his way in dry as she screamed to the sky. For help. For mercy. For anything.

Shades whimpered and grunted like a dying dog as he came in Herman's ass. He pushed off on the ground with both hands and rolled back onto his ass in violent satisfaction. Herman's hole made a suctioned POP when Shades' dick left the premises. A streak of shit gurgled out of Amanda's brother's ass with a creaking fart.

"Fuuuuuuuck. Man, that was intense. Fucker felt like your sister, big guy."

Fuck Yeah gave Shades the thumbs up as he relentlessly dry-fucked Amanda.

"You got any shit on your dick, Shades?" Debbie asked with supreme impatience.

"She wants the chili dog, huh?" Shades grinned evilly. He checked and sure enough, there was a healthy glob on his second head. With that bit of peanut butter-tinged fecal matter topping Shades' dick, he excitedly walked over to where Fuck Yeah pumped away in Amanda.

"You ready for that hotdog you didn't want to try earlier, bitch?"

Shades squatted down to his knees and tried several times to insert his dick in Amanda's mouth, but her body flailed all over the place as Fuck Yeah plowed her into oblivion. A nearby football tee used for kickoffs offered a solution. Shades grabbed it and used it to dislocate Amanda's jaw with an agonizingly long wet cracking sound. Now her mouth was open just enough for what he needed. He jammed his shit-smeared cock as far down her throat as he could, burying it to its hilt. Amanda was long past unconsciousness at this point.

Debbie relished in her Eighties men following her orders and obeying her every command. It made her wet like clockwork. She slowly and very ceremoniously stripped naked and fingered herself right there on the forty yard line to appreciative hoots and hollers from Shades and Fuck Yeah. Herman was out but still breathing, and his dick was hard of all things, poking out from the side of his belly like a scared prairie dog. The sight of Amanda getting action from two studs like Fuck Yeah and Shades made her want more. More of everything.

"Some nerd dick sounds good right about now, boys."

"Hell yeah, get some, baby!" Shades hollered.

"Fuck yeah, fuck yeah! Fuck yeah!"

Debbie made her way over to Herman, rolled him onto his back and spit on his three quarters hard dick. She stroked it until it was four quarters hard, threw a leg over him, lined herself up nice and even and lowered onto Herman's member as it slid in like it was nothing. She rode slow at first, knowing this nerd would probably spurt after three solid pumps. So she just wiggled around a little, trying to get some much-needed quality time on her G spot with the dork's decently sized dork.

"Not bad, not bad, loser. But let's see how you do under pressure. She went into mechanical bull mode and rode Herman hard as she choked him with both hands.

"Ain't this the life?" Shades wondered out loud.

Fuck Yeah agreed in the usual way and Debbie just laughed and laughed, cackling loud and long to the moon and stars.

Soon after, Fuck Yeah filled Amanda's womb like an overflowing milkshake, and Shade had emptied his baby batter in her mouth; shit mixed with cum in her gullet. Debbie let go of her stranglehold on Herman's neck as she came hard. Seconds later, cum spurted out the sides of Debbie's meat flaps like a busted dam. Herman lasted longer than she thought. Probably a chronic masturbator. The whole bottom half of Herman's body was soaking wet.

"Oh fuck, make me cum you fucking stupid nerd. That's right. The Hoover Fucking Dam ain't got shit on this freshly poured concrete pussy."

Fuck Yeah, enraptured with how much fun Debbie was having with Herman (and noticing how wet she was) picked Debbie up by the waist off of Herman's dick, clenched his fist, and rammed it up Herman's ass to stretch it out. Then, the lummox sat directly on Herman's hard prick.

"Oh fuck yeah, fuck yeah…"

Fuck yeah bounced so hard on Herman's dick there was soon a loud CRRRACK. He had broken Herman's pelvis.

Debbie, not being finished with Herman and still dripping out her cooch like a broken water hose, found a marching band baton lying nearby. Probably left there by one of one of the color guard teenie bopper skanks practicing earlier. It took about twenty swings to Fuck Yeah's head to make him stop riding the dented and damaged nerd. Fuck Yeah stood up and drunkenly staggered up and down the field butt naked as shit crept down his leg and blood dripped from a cut hid beneath his mullet thanks to Debbie's baton massage. Shades mocked him,

"You big beefy queer fuck! I knew you would take it in the ass sooner or later, ha ha ha!

Fuck Yeah seemingly agreed with Shades. "Oh fuck yeah, fuck yeah…"

The night had worn out its welcome for Debbie and she was ready to hit the bricks. Amanda and Herman were essentially dead to the world, barely breathing. It was time for the Eighties to pack up and roll out. Fuck Yeah eventually came to what little senses he had and returned to Debbie's side. Shades broke into the concession stand, grabbed a couple of candy bars, downed two or three Cokes, and rewrapped his swollen dick with a fresh ice pack.

Debbie wasn't too much worried about Amanda or Herman ratting either of them out whatsoever. Who would they report it to? Sheriff Dutra? That's a good one. She stood over Amanda's lifeless, shit, cum, blood and piss-stained body and spat on her.

"Welcome to Dutra High, new bitch. No one fucks with The Eighties."

All three made for the parking lot, jumped in Shades' Trans Am, and peeled out, leaving heavy black skid marks.

"Chili dogs are on me, boys!" Debbie said as she high fived both of her men repeatedly.

*****

Since the stadium lights were on a timer, they cut off a few hours after The Eighties left. It was now pitch black and the only soul stirring was Janitor Johnny. It was time for his nightly six mile run around the track and a rigorous workout that lasted for well over three hours. Ending just in time for the school day to begin after a bracing cold shower. Johnny walked on to the field with only a pair of jogging shorts and tennis shoes. Shirts were a hindrance to his easily chafed nipples. Especially at night. He was lean and ripped for a man of his age. Clothing hid it well during the day, but at night there were no secrets kept between his vascularity and the night sky. The only indicator on his body of being truly old was that salt-and-pepper beard and several scars from a forgotten time.

Off in the distance, in the blackness, a faint moan pierced the quiet. It startled Johnny to the point where he positioned himself in a combat stance that was only taught in self-defense and martial arts classes.

"Halt, or I will be forced to unleash my fury on those who attempt to do me harm!"

The sounds persisted. Who or whatever was cloaked by a thick fog that had settled on the football field right before morning. Soon, though, the form was revealed. It was Amanda. She was naked and bruised all over. Blood dripped down her inner thigh as she reached for Johnny. Her mouth was open, but no sounds came out anymore. What wasn't covered in blood was matted with sod, grass, and dirt. As best as Johnny could tell, she was trying to scream for help. To his horror, he saw that her jaw just hung open, the corners of her mouth ripped and torn. Blood smeared all over the lower half of her face. Amanda collapsed in front of Johnny. He could see there was nothing left inside of her. The wise-beyond-his-years janitor knew exactly who was responsible for this.

"I've got you now. It's okay. I promise."

Amanda tried to say something to him, but it came out as barely intelligible mumblings.

"Mah… Brovvv… Urmmm… Ovrrrr…"

And then she was gone.

The football field. Was there someone else out there? Johnny scooped up Amanda and carried her in his arms as he jogged into the murkiness of the darkened field. After a few moments of searching, he spotted a pale splotch of something on the ground, several yards ahead.

"Broth...? Your brother, sweetie?"

There was no answer from Amanda. She was beyond any help that could be offered out here.

Johnny made his way over to Herman and gasped. The boy looked like he had been ejected from a head-on collision. Blood was everywhere. He looked dead. Johnny looked down at the lifeless girl in his arms as a tear escaped his wrinkled face.

"I found him, sweetie. I found him."

PART TWO
THE FREAKS COME OUT AT NIGHT

CHAPTER VI

One year to the day passed, and every single day of that year was a literal Hell on Earth for both Amanda and Herman Masterson.

Johnny had located Amanda's phone after he found Herman that night and called 911. He waited as long as he could with them, but when EMS services arrived, he was nowhere to be found. In the wake of the attack, not one investigation was opened. Sheriff Dutra and his men never looked into the matter. Uncle Will was neither shocked nor surprised at the lack of concern for his niece and nephew. He just went about the business of taking care of them and helping them recover while he tried his best to keep Dutra High safe and clean. As safe and as clean as you could while Debbie Dutra and The Eighties roamed the halls.

The road to recovery was nearly impossible, especially for Amanda. She bled from her vaginal walls and esophagus almost every day. It was so bad that the docs at Dutra Memorial Hospital placed her in a medically induced coma to aid in uninterrupted recovery for nearly three months. After her revival, psychiatrists and speech therapists exhausted all efforts to get her to talk. Physical therapists visited her house to teach her how to walk again. It was no use. So she remained in a wheelchair, ate very little, and was catatonic most of the time. The only time she showed any emotion was when Uncle Will encouraged her to go back to school. That resulted in uncontrollable tantrums, screaming, crying, and violently slamming her head against the wall. Neither Herman nor Uncle Will could do anything to ease her pain.

As for Herman, his physical injuries seemed much worse than his psychological ones. His broken pelvis and torn anal cavity thanks to Fuck Yeah on top of his savage beating at the hands of Shades resulted in a body cast for the better part of the same three months Amanda was in a coma. Cosmetic dental surgery to repair his teeth resulted in a goofy, almost bucktooth bridge that concealed the oral trauma he suffered that night. Unable to comfort his shell-shocked sister, his only solace was obsessively watching his extensive collection of werewolf movies every day. Even An American Werewolf in Paris and Cursed. So deep was his compulsion. His obsession grew to be most unhealthy. He would aggressively and repeatedly jerk off to any of his movies where the wolf was tearing apart a human, all while wearing his trusty rubber werewolf mask.

For the most part, Uncle Will understood his trauma, but he knew it was time for him to face reality. A new school year was upon them all and that meant facing the corruption of the Dutras head-on yet again. If Amanda wasn't going to go, it was up to Will to keep an eye out for Herman once he returned.

A moment of clarity overcame Herman one night while watching Teen Wolf with Michael J. Fox for the twentieth time. He thought to himself, when Scott Howard transformed into a werewolf, he was invincible and wasn't scared of anyone.

"I would thell my thoul to the devil himthelf if I could become a werewolf."

He didn't even hear the fairly close crack of thunder followed by a brief yet blinding glint of lightning immediately after he uttered those words in his quiet, pitch-black bedroom. He was too busy stroking it to Susan Ursitti.

The first day of school for Herman had arrived yet again and Halloween was right around the corner. He had put it off long enough and Uncle Will had put his foot down about going back come mid-October. It was the cutoff for still being able to complete eleventh grade. His traumatic ordeal had been surprisingly and thoughtfully considered by Principal Lipshitz and the school board and their ultimate ruling was he could skip tenth grade. Herman wore his werewolf mask to school hoping it would give him some sort of supernatural power, courage, or at the least avoid the Eighties altogether. Maybe they wouldn't see through his disguise. Though his wounds had healed, he still had problems holding in his shit for more than a few minutes and he walked with a slight, wobbling limp. Unavoidable due to being turned into a bouncey house courtesy of Fuck Yeah. Herman fantasized about tearing through The Eighties with both claw and tooth many a lonely night in bed. He never brought it all the way to sexual fantasy, but it came really close, in a manner of speaking.

Back to school. Time to be a man. Whatever that meant.

*****

Uncle Will gave Herman a ride to school that morning. Not once did he tell him he had to remove the mask, even though he really wanted to. Herman wanted to get out at the curb in front of the school entrance but Will refused. He insisted on walking him inside once they had parked. Herman didn't say anything back. Just nodded. It was understood that they loved each other, and Will was just looking out for him. Words felt cheap lately. And completely unnecessary.

Before Uncle Will could even make it inside the building for his initial rounds with a masked Herman in tow, he busted a familiar teenage offender. Damian Wilson was a goth kid stereotype complete with black fingernails, dyed red hair, all-black wardrobe, and dark purple eyeliner.

He was utterly blitzed out in the driver's seat of his parents' faded grey '99 Oldsmobile Cutlass. Underneath him, a puddle of piss had formed. The corners of the perpetually troubled teen's mouth were crusted white and dried out. A needle was jammed in the crook of his left arm. The Eighties had undoubtedly hooked the misunderstood kid up with the absolute best heroin around yet again.

Uncle Will opened the door and pulled Damian out. There was no use in reporting it to Principal Lipshitz. It was already well known that the heroin was supplied by Debbie and the only way she could get away with it was with help from the school's administration.

Uncle Will dialed 911, hoping Damian would rat on who sold him the drugs after a nice stiff detox. Maybe this would be the beginning of the end to the drug-fueled rule of The Eighties.

One thing did give Will pause, though. Damian would probably be severely punished by his stepfather, Kirk Billingsley. A terrible, reprehensible man that got his rocks off by beating the hell out of Damian for the smallest infraction. The side effects of H were a lot easier to deal with than a belt buckle to the back for what seemed like an eternity.

It took Will and the arriving deputy to subdue the combative and surprisingly strong adolescent. He was likely a lot more afraid of his stepdad than the authorities.

Herman attempted to talk to Damian through his werewolf mask and his persistent speech impediment.

"Juth tell the polithe who you got the drugth from. My uncle ith a good guy and he will help you. I promith."

"Go to hell, you hair-lipped freak! You actually think a rubber mask will save you from what's about to come?! Fuck you, fuck your uncle, and fuck the world!"

The deputy hogtied Damian and threw him in the back of the squad car. He spat and kicked at the windows until his H-addled body ran out of gas. The squad car drove off, leaving both Will and Herman to wonder if they had done the right thing. Uncle Will gave Herman a firm pat on the back as they quietly went their separate ways.

*****

Herman's first class of the day was currently occupied by Debbie and Dewey Hammond. Apparently, The Eighties held up a liquor store over the summer and maimed the cashier on duty with a shotgun blast to the kneecap. Instead of doing jail time, Sheriff Dutra convinced the DA to allow them community service and to repeat their last grade over again. The benefits of having a caring, attentive father.

Herman limped into the room, saw both of them, and froze solid. Old memories and fear struck back at him. Debbie grabbed her pen, got Dewey's attention, and licked it up and down while looking at the hideous blob of excrement indicating a blow job that would not be given later. Instantaneously Dewey came up with the horrid chant of "Herman hair lip, Herman hair lip…" The whole class joined in, chanting the words in unison and pounding their fists on their desks. Apparently, his disguise wasn't as effective as Herman had hoped it would be.

The only person who wasn't joining in on the ridicule was their new teacher, a Ms. Sasha. It said so on the blackboard. She looked to be in her early thirties, five foot eight, a hundred thirty pounds or so, shoulder-length wavy black hair, a set of long, toned legs that were snug tight in black stockings; the kind that had the line that ran down the back of it, a pair of cherry red pumps, and a black leather skirt that stopped not too far from the bottom of her ass cheeks. Her figure was a perfect fifteen and was equipped with a little bit more than a handful of titties, and an ass you could sit a piping hot cup of coffee on.

Ms. Sasha frowned as soon as she noticed the humiliation in Herman's eyes. Herman ran to the bathroom, head hung low in disappointment. The classroom continued to chant until Ms. Sasha snapped her fingers. An instant silence blanketed the room, as if she had them in a trance; even Debbie. Now with the class completely silent, Ms. Sasha followed Herman to the bathroom.

Inside the little boy's room, Herman stood at one of the urinals trying to piss. The door opened with only one meager creak of its hinges. Herman heard the heels of Ms. Sasha's pumps click and clack on the porcelain-tiled bathroom floor. Why was she in here? The little girl's room was down the hall!

Ms. Sasha slowly walked up behind Herman, reached her hand around, cupped both of his balls, and gently whispered, "I know what you truly desire, Herman Masterson."

Herman flinched hard, zipped up, and backed away from Sasha quickly.

"Who-what… how do you know what I want, Mith…?"

Fresh piss recently dribbled on the floor caused Herman to lose his balance, and land flat on his back.

"Ms. Sasha, Herman my boy. Looks like you need to watch your step."

No man or woman on Earth or in any other dimension for that matter had ever turned Ms. Sasha down. It was time to bring in the big guns; her wet, hot, Venus fly trap. The sultry slut straddled Herman by standing directly over his face, exposing her freshly shaved muff. Hot pussy juices dripped onto Herman's face not unlike burning candle wax.

It singed Herman's skin as kisses of smoke rose up slowly. Seductively.

"Ouch, that burnth a little, ma'am!" Herman said, wiping his face.

"Oh, it gets hotter, Hermy."

"Wait… Only Amanda calth me—"

Without warning, Herman's pointer and middle finger fused together and formed a small penis. The fleshy dildo-finger inched toward Sasha's gash. Small, steamy vapor clouds oozed out of her hotter-than-Hell cooch. Herman's dick finger slid in easily and worked its way back and forth vigorously.

"Oh yeah, Hermy, that's it right there. You're sooo goood at this!"

"What… What are you doing to me—"

Herman tried to pull out, but Sasha's clam trap tightened its grip into a vice. He was in for the long haul like it or not. Moans of ecstasy echoed throughout the halls for the next three minutes. Herman screamed in excruciating pain as his dick finger received some lovely first-degree burns.

An unfortunate male teen ran in holding his crotch, toting a full pissbag. It breaks Sasha's concentration, which allowed Herman to yank his fingers away from her furnace flaps. She pointed to the desperate boy and with her mind fuckery, commanded the boy to unzip and unload his pee hose directly into his own mouth, trying in vain to drink all of his own warm lemonade. After he was empty, he ran screaming and puking back out into the hallway.

"Now, where were we?"

Herman jumped up, ran into a bathroom stall, and locked the door. His fingers had returned to their separate selves. But now painful welts filled with pus covered them.

Sasha's bifurcated tongue lashed out and snaked its way underneath his stall. It slithered up Herman's pants leg, and right up to his mouth. Herman clamped down and gritted his teeth, trying to deny her tongue entry. It was no use. Her python tongue easily pried open his mouth as he screamed in terror. The pink, throbbing fleshy muscle snuck its way past his teeth and headed towards his lungs. Herman could barely breathe with her snakey mouth probe already partially blocking his airway.

"Tonight. Midnight. Where it all began a year ago. Your pain, your suffering. It can all be reversed. I know your deepest wish, your most coveted desire. It will be granted, my little man. Do you believe me?"

Herman nodded weakly.

Unconvinced, Ms. Sasha continued her tongue's march down Herman's throat.

"Okay, okay, I'll be there. I promith! Pleath!" Herman squealed, trying to gasp for air but just gagging on her suffocating tongue.

Then, just like that, her tongue retracted and all was as it was before. Herman gasped for air, massaging his throat then flung open the stall door. Ms. Sasha was gone.

For the rest of the day, Herman remained in the stall, afraid and extremely confused. As the day progressed, he put two and two together. Did his late-night, bedtime wish to be a werewolf have something to do with Ms. Sasha showing up out of nowhere? Or was it all a dream? A hallucination brought on by trauma? His therapist said things like this might happen. That had to be it.

*****

Night had slowly crept in, and Herman still cowered in the bathroom. The only thing that brought him out was a startling gunshot from outside. Lying in the darkness of the night was a shape cloaked in a ghillie suit. The type a military sniper would usually wear. All Herman could make out through the murky bathroom window was a muzzle flash going off once every thirty seconds. He counted nineteen in all. The weird thing was whoever it was seemingly didn't have any type of actual rifle. It looked as if the muzzle flash was coming directly from his hands. This went on for several minutes until the unknown figure stood up and was revealed to be Janitor Johnny. He looked around and stopped his gaze directly at the window Herman was looking out of, which made the boy flinch and back away. When he regained enough composure to look again, the janitor was nowhere to be spotted.

It wasn't until Herman could safely make it across the empty parking lot could he discover just what Johnny was shooting at. There were no lights around and clouds partially covered the moon. Virtually pitch black. In his search, Herman tripped and fell to the asphalt. Right there before his eyes were the remains of nineteen shattered longneck beer bottles. As best as he could tell, each bottle had a cut-out piece of paper with a face on it. Each face was that of Sheriff Dutra, and each piece had a single bullet hole right between the eyes. He recognized the Sheriff's face from the ugly billboard displayed on the side of the road coming into town for the first time. What did the school janitor have to do with the Sheriff? How could he have blasted nineteen bottles with deadly accuracy, not missing one time, from more than a hundred yards, and in complete darkness? And with no weapon? All these questions raced through Herman's mind as he made his way home.

CHAPTER VII

Uncle Will waited in silence at the kitchen table for Herman. The masked teen tried to sneak by without having to talk to his uncle, but Will heard the door squeak and stopped him in his tracks with just his voice.

"Home kinda late. Everything okay?"

"No, it's not okay. I had to hide in the bathroom again hoping Debbie wasn't hanging around to finish the job!" Herman yelled angrily.

"I'm sorry. It was my job to keep you safe and I couldn't. Didn't," Will said in a dreadful tone as he hung his head shamefully.

"Thorry Unc, I didn't mean to yell."

"No, you're right Herman it's not okay. Something's gotta be done about that she-devil and her posse once and for all."

Herman began to cry through his worn, rubbery werewolf mask.

"Where were you? I needed you. Amanda needed you."

Will grabbed his nephew and hugged him as tight as he could. "I'll make everything right. I promise. I know what needs to be done now."

"Whatever…" Herman broke free from Will and ran to his sister's bedroom.

Amanda sat on the edge of her bed, staring aimlessly out the window. Herman could do nothing to ease her pain. He felt useless. Impotent. There was no acknowledgment of his presence on her part. Not expecting a response after so long, Herman asked her, "What do you want me to do, thith? I'm juth too weak to fight back and Uncle Will ith only going to make thingth worth."

Amanda turned to Herman, gave a slight and weak smile, then mouthed the words "Kill them." It was a most unexpected response, and it made the hairs on Herman's arms stand straight up.

Herman looked out the window into the cool, dark night air and gave a small nod. Though he was afraid of the crazy woman in the bathroom, it was almost time to meet this Ms. Sasha on the football field. That field. It gave him the shakes just thinking about it. On top of that, there was no guarantee of what was about to happen at all. But considering all the bad luck brought upon him and his sister, he was game for whatever. He'd meet her for Amanda. What was the worst that could happen? Another lonely walk home after being pranked by the new teacher. The new, hot teacher. Herman's dick got a little hard thinking about Ms. Sasha. Her body. Her voice. The way she was in charge at all times. He hated to admit it, but she turned him on more than she should given the situation.

Uncle Will was passed out on the couch and deep in a loop of heavy snoring and REM sleep. Herman tiptoed as best he could with his limp, hoping not to wake him. A waxing gibbous moon provided the eager teenager with just enough illumination to lead the way to the accursed football field.

*****

The stadium's high beams lit up an empty, scarily quiet football field. Even the droning buzz of the lights seemed muffled for some reason.

As he took the field proper, no one came forth to meet him. He was all by his sad sack lonesome self.

Herman muttered to himself, "Damn, I knew it wath too good to be true."

His barely subconscious desire to see Ms. Sasha again in the flesh was apparently not on the schedule for tonight after all.

"Oh well," Herman told himself as he walked, head hung in the usual position.

But before he could step off the football field all the way, a smooth-as-silk and deadly-sharp voice echoed over the stadium loudspeakers.

"Are you happy?"

Then an ear-piercing maniacal laugh echoed throughout the area.

"Born October thirtieth, 2006. Father and mother traded him and his sister for illegal pharmaceuticals. For the next fifteen years he was sodomized, beaten, and used as a means of sexual gratification. And frustration. Yikes."

Herman flinched. He reached for his mask, still on his face. Instead of taking it off, he made sure it was on extra tight. She was here after all. He couldn't let her see his fear.

Werewolf up, Herman. Werewolf up.

"Sister Amanda Masterson, quite similar life experience. Except for the surprise pregnancy, of course. Pity."

Several seconds of silence followed.

In that silence, Ms. Sasha walked out from the press box and down the bleachers. As she did, the flowing, deep purple silk kimono she wore slid its way off her frame as if in slow motion. There was his new teacher, completely naked. Her body was beyond glorious. Every hetero teenage boy's dream of what a gorgeous woman should look like. Her tits didn't bounce too much, and her ass bounced even more than any young cock could handle. Herman shook his head, and pinched himself to make sure he wasn't dreaming. The pinch hurt. He pushed against his rising cock through his pants, hoping she wouldn't see his inescapable erection.

The first words out of Ms. Sasha's mouth as her hot cherry and perfectly pedicured red-painted toenails stepped onto the field were, "Been shitting regularly lately?"

"That dependth. Have you molethted anymore underage boyth in a public bathroom?"

He was trying so hard to be brave. For Amanda. For himself. But his lisp made it a nearly impossible task. Especially in front of such insurmountable arousal.

Sasha's tongue slithered out of her mouth. The tip encircled her left nipple. She looked up and giggled.

"More than I can count."

Sasha switched to a more matter-of-fact tone as she looked Herman up and down nice and slow.

"Did you know Shades throat fucked your sister until she couldn't speak? And that Deborah Dutra raped you while you were unconscious? Because they did, sweetie."

Those horrendous bits of information paused his erection in its tracks.

"Why tell me that now? And how do you know that? Whath the catch to all of thith?"

"Oh, there's definitely a catch."

Ms. Sasha spread her legs apart a few inches and smiled playfully, which still came across as pure evil to Herman.

"My pussy needs more of your dick fingers, Hermy."

Herman's eyes crossed, and his teeth gritted in a painful grimace. There were still several blisters on his fingers from his last visit to Ms. Sasha's 212-degree Fahrenheit stench trench.

"Sit…" She commanded him with a finger pointing at the ground.

Herman felt compelled to sit right away, her voice like a lubricant to his returning erection. So he sat down on the ground and adjusted his mask once more.

"Good dog."

She placed her bare foot directly on Herman's crotch. Each cherry-tipped digit wiggled independently and vibrated simultaneously around his ball sac region.

"You like that?"

Herman was frozen in inescapable pleasure. "Why do I all of a thudden have a foot fetith?"

"It's really quite simple. Each of my toes is like five pussies and all five want to fuck you into a deal with the head honcho."

Herman shook his head in confusion, while still enjoying the greatest foot job ever.

"Tho, I give youth my thoul and you make me a demon?

"Interested, Hermy? I just need your verbal consent and we can make all your dreams come true. Sex. Revenge. Respect. Manhood. The whole bag of marbles."

Herman never thought of himself as a foot man, but it was hard to resist the perfect form of her feet. Both arches were smooth as warm butter. Each toe was perfectly proportioned. The smoothness of the soles was like the bottom of a baby's ass. As Ms. Sasha's nimble toes unzipped Herman's pants and pulled out his now rock-hard cock through his strained boxers, his eyes rolled into the back of his head. He was, however, able to ask one lucid question.

"Do I get to kill The Eightieth?"

"Oh yes my dear, absolutely. But upon your eventual death, whenever that may be, your soul will be mine."

"Huh. Do… I get more footjobs?"

"As many as your fragile flesh desires."

"Thure. It's a deal. Can I be a werewolf?"

Ms. Sasha laughed heartily and clapped her hands.

"I thought you'd never ask!"

Sasha's feet completely covered Herman's dick in pure ecstasy. She stroked his throbbing, veiny penis between the soft arches of her feet. Lotion seemed to secrete out of her very pores, lubing up Herman's dick and sending it to inhuman levels of pleasure. The sounds of squishy, wet, demon-made aloe vera and lanolin oozed and gushed onto Herman's shaft and nutsack. Lotion embedded into his pubic hairs. Small bits of precum squirted out of the tip of his pecker.

Fangs soon protruded through Herman's gums, sending blood squirting out of the corners of his wide-open mouth. As she sped up, his eyes turned yellow, and he could hear at least a hundred times better than a human. He could now hear someone hiding in the tunnel leading to the locker rooms. Someone fat and wheezy. Someone scared out of their mind. He could barely concentrate on anything apart from the ecstasy his dick was feeling right then and there.

The deal was finally sealed as Herman spunked all over Sasha's feet. His first werewolf howl came from somewhere deep down in his diaphragm. He ripped off his flimsy werewolf mask as his face mirrored the real deal.

"Awoooooooooooo!"

Sasha grabbed both her feet and licked off the mixture of lotion and boyonaise until her red-painted toenails were shining once again in the Friday night lights.

"Mmmmm. Restaurant quality, Hermy. A deal's a deal."

Muffled screams came from the tunnel. Someone terrified and unable to hold it in anymore. It caused great pain to Herman's new heightened sense of hearing.

"Who is that?!" He yelled out in a deep, growly voice.

Sasha pointed to the dark, shadowy tunnel with a long, clawed finger.

"Come forth, human excrement!"

Dewey Wilcox waddled into the light, gagged with a sweaty, piss-stained jock strap, arms tied behind the back, nude from the waist down, his fat, flabby giggling gut covering his thimble wiener. A hellish force compelled Dewey to walk with contorted robot movements towards Herman and Ms. Sasha. He stopped in front of Herman and mumbled through his gag, "I'm sorry Herman. Please don't kill me."

To add a little insult to injury, Ms. Sasha flicked her wrist and every pimple, blackhead, whitehead, and all other filled pores on Dewey's face popped all at once. Dewey squinted his eyes in agony as pus, oil, dirt, and patches of pustules covered his face in a drippy puddle of gunk.

Sasha laughed at the grotesque merriment.

"Wow, haven't seen that much boy batter since I jerked off an entire little league baseball team back in '99!"

Her eyes rolled in the back of her head as she bit her lower lip in nostalgic ecstasy.

"Can't wait for 'em to arrive in hell. They all wanted to be ninjas or some stupid shit. I'll have every one of those little pissants running a train on my flesh scrunchie."

"Um. What?"

"Oh yeah, cut a deal with every one of those little shits. Come to find out the coach had a fetish for little boys. He was fucking them in the ass then felch—"

"Please, stop. I get it. Wait a minute… My lisp. It's—"

Ms. Sasha took the ball gag out of Dewey's mouth to let him plead for his life one more time "Herman, please don't do this. All I ever wanted was to be cool, you know, be accepted. Just like you, man. Look at me, I'm a fucking loser, my face looks like pepperoni pizza, and I have no friends. I'll talk to The Eighties. You know, smooth things over. They'll listen to me! I swear!"

"No, they won't Dewey. They're evil and that's that. As long as you're alive you'll continue to do whatever they tell you."

Ms. Sasha pulled a baseball bat out of her vagina and handed it to Herman.

"Where did that come from?"

"My pussy, Herman. Do you have eyes or what?"

He took it and promptly broke the handle off with his newfound werewolf strength and told Dewey through a grimaced and painful expression, "You're going to feel what my sister felt that night and soon The Eighties will as well."

Dewey's peepers grew wide; he wailed out in excruciating pain as the fat end of the baseball bat was shoved up his ass. An unmistakable shit smell wafted through the brisk late-night air. Only the broken nub end of the bat was sticking out of his rectum. The splintered end wiggled about furiously as Dewey ran around in a circle, begging for relief

"Get it out, get it out, please!"

Ms. Sasha congratulated Herman with a long, sensual, and sloppy French kiss while squeezing his ass cheeks. Herman's eyes lit up with delight. This was Herman's first kiss by the sexiest bitch in Heaven, Hell, or on Earth.

Herman eventually managed to dislodge Sasha's long tongue from his stomach. At least that's where it felt like it ended up anyways. As Dewey was making his way to the stadium exit, Herman crept up behind him. Shit and blood squirted out of Dewey's asshole with every spastic movement. Whatever Herman was about to do from now on in the name of revenge would have to be greater than or equal to the torment he and his sister encountered on that very same football field one year ago.

Herman didn't have to do much more as Dewey soon seized all functions of body, mind, and soul. He went face-first into a pile of dogshit that was already swarming with a bevy of flies. With a hard werewolf kick, Herman sent the baseball bat all the way up Dewey's ass, past his intestines, and out through his stomach.

Sasha attempted to further congratulate Herman with another kiss, but Herman stopped her with a firm hand on her chest.

"Uh, is it possible to hold off on the roto-rootering of my esophagus until I get rid of the rest of them?"

"What are you gay now? Maybe you enjoyed shoving that bat up Dewey's ass a little too much if you know what I mean. I can be a man if that's what you want. What's your preference? Twink? Bear? A little of both?"

"Did you use that pickup line on the little league team back in '99? And what's with the gay stuff? You're the one who gave me the bat."

"To beat him to death with!"

"Oh. Right."

"You're getting funnier the more hair grows on your balls, Hermy. Your sister would be into you now, I bet. What a stud!"

"Is everything a sex thing with you? Are you ever satisfied?"

"I'm a fucking succubus, Hermy. A lust demon. So, no."

Sasha clicked her tongue and shifted her eyes from left to right as hot ashen vapors screamed from her vagina.

"Yeah, you know, Satan, they can go downtown to Chinatown, make three shrimp eggrolls, tickle the octopussy, and leave me satisfied for a week and a half. At least."

"Can they teach me how to do that?"

"All in due time, sweetie…"

And then, Sasha disappeared into the ground. The only evidence of her even being there was a couple patches of singed grass and a lone dark purple kimono lightly rippling in the breeze near the bleachers.

Herman strolled off the field full of life and anxious to fulfill his lifelong dream of being a werewolf. A predator of the night fueled by revenge, anger, and every werewolf movie committed to the silver screen, DVD, or hell, even straight to VHS.

CHAPTER VIII

It was now two days before Halloween, and on the surface, all seemed quiet.

Uncle Will made it a point to arrive early to school with Herman to make his rounds and help Herman avoid running into The Eighties in the parking lot.

But on this morning, Herman knew exactly what his uncle would find on the ballfield. There was Dewey, already on an express trip to Rot Town. Flies buzzed and swarmed around the rancid and discolored blob of a corpse. Will had to shoo off a pair of vultures that were pecking away at the wannabe bully's intestines. Off in the distance, Herman was peeking from behind a set of bleachers, admiring his handy work while Will called 911. Herman tried really hard to look surprised. He even wore his mask to school to keep his uncle from suspecting anything different about him.

The sun was up a considerable amount, and it was nearing time for school to start. Only two sheriff's vehicles showed up. One was Sheriff Raymond Dutra and the other was Sheriff's Deputy Colin Elam. Elam immediately began taping off the crime scene. That was until Sheriff Dutra stopped him with a poke to the ribs.

"What the goddamn hell are you doing, boy? That tape is fourteen ninety-nine a roll. We're pigshit in the middle of budget cuts you broken barrel of stupid!"

Deputy Elam almost jumped out of his boots as Sheriff Dutra chewed a hole in his left ass cheek.

Raymond Weston Dutra strutted around the crime scene with his proud, southern game cock ego, boisterous beer gut, ten-gallon hat, alligator skin boots equipped with spurs, and a holstered Smith & Wesson Model 500m revolver. 60,000 psi. That piece of twisted steel was pure, unadulterated, brain-splattering power. The lack of remorse for Dewey was noted as Dutra addressed Sgt. Elam with a thick southern twang.

"I'd say it's almost a goddamned shame this summabitch is dead, but I'd be a lyin' whore in church, now wouldn't I, dep-u-tee?"

As Sheriff Dutra grinned wide, the honorable deputy gagged and coughed to beat the band, barely nodding in agreement with his boss.

Sheriff Dutra poked and prodded the corpse with his size fourteen boot. A brown, putrid sludge oozed from Dewey's every orifice. It only took three minutes tops for Dutra to determine a cause of death.

"Looks like natural causes to me. Bag and tag this lump of shit, Elam. I'm missing my free complimentary pancake and meat lover's breakfast skillet down at Ima Jean's Café as we speak. Need to get my biscuits buttered if you know what I mean."

"Ten-four, Sheriff," Elam sighed.

As Dutra vacated the crime scene, he passed by Will. The security guard stared skeptically at the Sheriff, who stopped right in front of him with a hand on his revolver.

"You got a fuckin' eyeball problem, Jameson?"

Will knew it was useless to argue with the headstrong bull of a man. Who was he to go up against the Dutra name? But he felt like he had to say something.

"Nice work closing the case here. Town can sleep safe now, I wager."

Will involuntarily placed a hand on his own holstered gun to emphasize his sarcasm. Dutra spotted it and frowned.

"You and I gonna have a chat about jurisdiction and boundaries some other time. I'm late for pancakes and titty squeezes."

"You say hi to Ima Jean for me, Sheriff."

Dutra eased his hand off his revolver and sidled onward to his vehicle, mumbling something about Will being a "funny fucker…"

About the same time the sheriff was hopping into his Blazer, his sweet little Debbie came prancing up.

"What happened, Daddy?"

"Aw hell, Little D, that fat fuckin' Wilcox kid got sodomized to everlovin' death with a Louisville Slugger it seems. You ain't knowin' nothing about that, yeah? Your boys do this?"

"Oh hell no, Daddy. Dewey was a fr—well, he was a groupie. Jesus Christ on a—"

The Sheriff gives his daughter a light smack on the cheek.

"What I tell you about that godforsaken blasphemy? Jesus can hear you when you shit sideways outta yer mouth like that!"

"Sorry, Daddy. I won't do it again. I promise."

"Would break your mother's heart to hear you talk about the Lord like such."

"Sorry. I swear."

"Now what can I do for you, my little lambcake?"

"Daddy, I don't know who did… whatever happened to Dewey, but I do know one thing."

"And that is…?"

"That security guard, he's always out to get me and I don't know why. I've never done anything to him. We've never done anything to him. He's the one who pointed his gun at me after that Masterson girl kicked me in the god d—"

Dutra eyes his daughter warily, cocking his head."

"I mean, she kicked me in the damn hoo hoo, Daddy!"

"Your hoo hoo? That a dessert cake, sugar?"

"No, Daddy. My, you know. My thing. She kicked me right in there. And laughed about it. Along with her freakonaut brother in the werewolf mask. They're all crazy and out to get me!"

"Don't worry about him none. You catch any more problems from his way, just call me, sugar plum. 'Kay?"

Debbie kissed Raymond Dutra with an open mouth, turned, and before she could walk away, the sheriff popped her on the ass. Debbie turned back, giggled briefly, then walked right into the school.

"Thank you, Daddy!" She called out as she entered the building. Shades and Fuck Yeah joined her just inside the entryway.

Sheriff Dutra shifted his already growing erection beneath his slacks as she watched her leave.

"God, if she weren't my daughter, I'd have her ass barefoot and pregnant toot sweet."

"That's incest, boss."

"Don't read shit from the rule book to me, Deputy. Just get back to the office and pronto."

Deputy Elam just nodded and stumbled back to his car.

*****

The first stop for Debbie was the principal's office. To keep selling H, Debbie had to tend to Lipshitz's lascivious libido like a prudent gardener tends to their flowers. To her surprise, Ms. Sasha was already conducting a little business with the perverted school official. Debbie peeked through the partially opened door. There she was with her tits pressed up against the backside of the principal's head and giving him a deep shoulder massage. In Debbie's warped mind, the principal was her property. The thought of another woman playing her game infuriated her. Massaging Lipshitz's neck seemed to put him in a state of indescribable euphoria. Debbie wanted so badly to interrupt but now was not the time apparently. Now she could blackmail the principal for whatever she wanted on account of him finding a new set of knockers to hang his hat on. Her dream of ruling the school with an iron fist and a wet hot pussy was still alive and well, no matter what this new twat teacher was up to lately. Debbie huffed off to her homeroom as she caught a glimpse of Ms. Sasha sneering at her.

*****

Herman cruised the halls loud and proud. All the kids pointed and whispered as he sauntered by. No limp and no mask once he was out of sight of his uncle. It was common knowledge that werewolves had a keen sense of smell and hearing. There was some automatic name-calling thrown Herman's way but most of the gossip was about Shades' legendary Halloween party. Everybody who was anybody at Dutra High would be there. It was an 80s-themed costume party, of course.

Off by herself was an attractive freshman girl rustling through her locker. Herman tiptoed up behind her. His nostrils flared out just enough to notice how sweet she smelled. He commented on it from the other side of the open locker door.

"Cherry lip balm?

The girl closed her locker and answered sweetly, "Nope, raspberry. Want some?"

"Does a one-legged duck swim in a circle?"

The smitten adolescent with perky tits generously smeared more than half of her raspberry lip gloss over her kissers in a slow circular motion, grabbed Herman by the neck, and kissed him for at least a good, dick-stiffening thirty seconds. After she finished, she licked what was left off of her lips and asked Herman, "Can we fuck sometime? I mean not like here and now but soon."

Herman felt so strong and virile. Conversation came easy now. Nothing made him anxious anymore. The school seemed like a playground waiting for him to hump the jungle gym now. It was such a freeing feeling. Sexy, too. Real fucking sexy.

"Of course, but first I need to do a little pest control. You cool with that, babe?"

Before the girl could answer, Herman walked off sporting a shit-eating grin with two partially protruding fangs.

The first one to truly notice Herman's newfound confidence beyond a surface level was Janitor Johnny. Usually, Herman could barely make eye contact with the old man. He passed by Johnny with a yellow-goldish tint in his eyes. Their eyes locked. Herman's confidence was indeed there in full force. However, Johnny had played this game before and had more wins than losses. Herman soon folded under the janitor's intimidating thousand-yard stare. Instead of scaring him, it intrigued him. He wanted to find out more about this guy.

Instead of retreating to the bathroom after the staring contest, Herman opened the door to Ms. Sasha's classroom. Debbie's oppressive presence did not phase the once meek and scared boy. Herman growled like an irate pit bull, then gave Debbie a loud and uproarious bark which made her jump and swear under her breath.

Ms. Sasha welcomed Herman to a brand-new day with a wink as he casually strolled back to his desk. It didn't take long for Chet to welcome him back to class with a hard flick to the left ear. It hurt like hell, but Herman would not give the big dumb lummox the satisfaction of knowing that. He ignored Captain Meathead and made it to his seat.

Chet, with his football helmet firmly on, stood up, and donkey-punched Herman in the back of the neck. That right there was the straw that broke the camel's back. Debbie screamed with laughter and flashed Chet her titties. Preoccupied with the sight of Debbie's fleshy mounds, Chet never saw Herman stand up and deliver a devastating left hook to his protected cranium. The helmet split in half and fell to the floor. The punch was so hard that it even cracked Chet's mouthguard and busted his nose.

Herman stood there with clenched teeth and clenched fists, looking at Chet with a yellow-eyed stare as blood poured from Chet's now severely deformed nose.

"Looks like you're gonna need something a little sturdier for next Friday's big game, huh?"

Debbie jumped up out of her seat, madder than a wet hen. Her voice shrilled in anger at Ms. Sasha.

"Did you just see what that spaz did to my boyfriend?! Hello?!"

Ms. Sasha's eyes glowed red and straight into Debbie's dark, corrupted soul.

"Sit down now, Ms. Dutra. Or should I just call you Debbie Downer?"

The whole class laughed at Ms. Sasha's joke, and all started chanting "Debbie Downer!" over and over again as Debbie's body grew stiff; her ass planted itself firmly into her seat, seemingly controlled by a snap of Ms. Sasha's perfectly manicured fingers.

Chet just sat there on the floor, embarrassed and holding his bloodied, broken nose with both hands. Ms. Sasha glanced at Herman with a sly smile.

"Mr. Masterson, you're excused for the rest of the day."

Still stuck in her seat, Debbie squealed in outrage.

"What the fuck? Why does Hair Lip get a hall pass? I wanna see the principal!"

Ms. Sasha laughed heartily at that.

"Oh, sweetie. That may be, but he doesn't want to see you."

*****

Herman strutted straight to the little boy's room. Yeah, he could have gone outside and pissed on a tree, but what better place to mark his territory than the busiest bathroom in the whole school? A place once reserved as a hiding spot for him was now his home turf. A trap to spring on unsuspecting bullies.

The door swung open and who of all people but Shades himself was right there, snorting a line of cocaine off one of the sinks. Fuck Yeah was taking a shit in the urinal and smoking a crooked joint. Without Debbie directing either one, every step of the way, they were as useless as a vibrator without a battery.

Any other time before last night, Herman would have tucked tail and ran in the other direction; but not anymore. Shades snorted the last line off the wet, soapy sink, cleared his throat, and turned to face the statue-still Herman with a furrowed brow and a toothy frown. Fuck Yeah struggled on the urinal to pinch off a loaf and dropped his joint right on his floppy donkey dick. He didn't even yelp in pain. Just a couple of "Oh fuck yeahs!"

"What time does the party start, Shades?" Herman asks him with a slight cock of his head.

Shades wiped the cocaine residue from his nose, licked his gums, lowered his glasses, and blinked his bloodshot eyes repeatedly.

"Not sure, Hermy. What time does your sister's pussy re-open?"

He followed that up with a finger on each side of his mouth and poked his flapping tongue through them.

Fuck Yeah plopped another log into the urinal and laughed out loud.

"Ohhhh fuck yeah, fuck yeah!"

A switchblade flipped out from Shades' balled left fist with a sharp SNIKT as he charged Herman from across the bathroom. Herman growled and snarled with a full set of fangs. Shades lunged his blade straight at Herman's chest but missed as Herman stepped aside with inhuman reflexes and snatched the blade from his hand. Shades' face crashed right into the mirror just above the sink. Shards of glass embedded in his forehead as he screamed every curse word in the English language and then some. Blood coated the front of his cracked sunglasses as he attempted to shake the cobwebs out from what was most likely a nasty concussion.

Herman tossed the knife up in the air, caught it by the handle, and buried the blade up to the hilt in Shades' left ass cheek.

"Goddamn punk ass honky! That shit hurts!"

Shades reached behind him and pulled out the blade. Blood oozed out of his ass like lava seeping out of a volcano.

Herman felt strong. Real strong. Scary strong. But he also still felt a bit like his old dorky self deep down. Not fully werewolfing out probably had something to do with it. Until the full moon arrived, he'd never be at full strength. It felt like his powers were still developing, like some kind of time-lapsed puberty on steroids.

Fuck Yeah finally jumped off the urinal to attack, but Herman bear-hugged him, lifted him off his feet, performed a backwards bodyslam over his head, and threw him into the first metal divider that separated the toilet stalls. The divider broke off its hinges with a loud crash as Fuck Yeah rocketed into it. The divider ultimately shattered the nearest toilet into hundreds of pieces. Water from it proceeded to flood the entire bathroom. There was

Fuck Yeah, smelling like stagnated piss from about ten other boys before him. Wadded up bits of toilet paper meshed with his now frizzled and unkempt mullet as he grabbed the porcelain lid to the toilet and with all his might threw it at Herman. Seconds before the lid could make contact BLAMMO! Herman punched straight thru the slab of white porcelain with his fist. It smashed into smithereens and a chunk of broken porcelain bounced off Fuck Yeah's head. Almost immediately, a golf ball-sized welt formed just above his left eye. Luckily for Fuck Yeah there wasn't much up there to protect.

Herman stood exhausted and breathing heavy, hoping both goons would realize it was time to retreat and regroup. Shades tried to hurl a snappy insult but one of his teeth spat out and landed on the floor. All he could do was point at Herman and whine, "I'm… I'm gonna get you, you… you fucking nerd!"

Fuck Yeah nodded vehemently at Shades, apparently agreeing with his frustration.

"Fuuuck yeahhh. Fuck… fuck yeah, yeah fuck yeah!"

"It's okay, buddy. Let's go guzzle a pony keg, watch some retard porn, and rub the poison out…"

Eyeing Herman all the way, Shades walked into the adjacent toilet stalls, now divider-less, with head hung low, yanked a roll of toilet paper off the dispenser, and held it against the back of his ass. It didn't take long for the toilet paper to resemble a used sanitary napkin.

As Fuck Yeah and Shades began to back out of the bathroom, Herman chuckled.

"I just wanted to know what time the party starts, boys. Gonna go as a werewolf. Cool, huh?"

His snarky tone only infuriated the two battered delinquents.

"You're dead, freakshow. You hear me? Next time we see you; you got a funeral coming your way! Fucking nerd-ass motherfucker!"

As they escaped the confines of their bathroom battlefield, they ran right into Janitor Johnny. He connected with a vicious roundhouse kick to Shades' face, followed by a spear hand to the sternum. Shades dropped to his knees with labored, wheezing respirations.

Before Fuck Yeah could retaliate for his friend, he witnessed Johnny perform a quite impressive show with a pair of nunchakus. Entranced, the big guy doesn't even try to block several nunchaku blows to his girthy midsection followed by two furious and dizzying strikes to each side of his massive cranium.

The newborn toilet-lid hematoma on Fuck Yeah's head exploded like a firecracker. Blood, clear liquid, and other fluids spewed from his forehead. Fuck Yeah fell to his knees and the old janitor smashed him in the mouth with a lightning-quick fist for the coup de gras. And the fight was over just like that.

"Your days of bullying defenseless teenagers are over. Satan will be defeated, and your souls will suffer for an eternity. For I am the great and mystical avenging one!"

Johnny then disappeared into a room labeled JANITOR'S CLOSET. On the other side of the door, water could be heard running. And then, as if nothing happened, Johnny returned with a mop bucket full of water, a wet floor sign, and a mop. He casually placed the sign near the boy's room, entered the bathroom, and began to clean up the flooded bathroom while whistling a melodic and upbeat tune.

CHAPTER IX

To both Uncle Will and Herman's surprise, the next day Amanda sat at the edge of her bed ready for school. It was the day before Halloween and the morning was aglow with the Fall atmosphere.

As always, she had on a simple but beautiful dress, her hair was back to its illustrious sheen, and the best part of all, there was a smile on her face.

"You have anything to do with this?"

"Nope. Not me, Unc," Herman said as he smiled back at Amanda.

"Well, it wasn't me, that's for sure."

"Maybe she's just ready."

Herman looked at Will then at Amanda. "You sure about this, sis?" Amanda still hadn't got her voice back, but it was a step in the right direction. She nodded her head up and down, stood up, did a flirty little twirl, and gave both Uncle Will and Herman a peck on the cheek. The subtle shade of pink lipstick she was wearing left a slight kiss imprint on each of their faces.

"You kids need a ride to school?" Will asked.

"You know, I think we can walk today. I have a feeling things are a little safer now," Herman said as he winked at Amanda.

She let out a smirky chuckle that was just above a faint whisper. Uncle Will and Herman were delighted to hear anything come out of her mouth.

Herman puffed out his chest and flexed his bicep to assure Will and Amanda from here on out he was, indeed, a brand new kinda guy.

*****

The morning stroll to school was as pleasant as could be. The leaves were falling from the trees right on schedule. Nearly every house they passed was decorated with pumpkins, spooky ghosts, and scary skeletons. Amanda and Herman held hands gleefully as the two enjoyed a moment of serenity.

Not far behind the two and getting closer was Shades at the wheel and Debbie riding shotgun in that hot ass red Trans-Am. "Hey Mickey" by Tony Basil blasted loud from the speakers. The car came to a screeching halt when Debbie yelled out to Amanda, "Pussy healed yet, new bitch?!"

Amanda did her level best to ignore Debbie, but Herman couldn't. Not anymore. Not after yesterday. He had them on the ropes. It was just a matter of time until they were done for. He stood stone still, dropped his book bag, and responded with supreme confidence.

"How many stitches did Shades need to fix his flat ass?"

The passenger car door swung open immediately, Debbie jumped out, and rushed up to Amanda, circling her repeatedly while singing along with Tony Basil.

"Oh Amanda, you're so fine, you're so fine you blow my mind, hey Amanda!"

Right at the last utterance of Amanda's name, Debbie brought forth a loogie with the utmost effort and spat it right into Amanda's face. Amanda screamed in terror. Her knees buckled and she fell to the ground and right into the fetal position.

Fuck Yeah appeared from behind a thick oak tree brandishing a baseball bat and whacked Herman over the head with all of his brute strength. The hit was so hard it broke the bat into two pieces. Herman thudded to the ground face first. Out cold.

Debbie pulled back her left high-heeled patent leather shoe like a pendulum and delivered a stiff kick with hellish force to Amanda's midsection. She gasped for air between hoarse, ear-piercing screams of terror. Herman remained unmoving and unconscious.

Shades stepped out from the driver's seat of his car, limped around to join the commotion with a still-sore ass, and soon noticed a dog squatting to take a shit. After the dog did his business, Shades snagged the juicy and freshly plopped pile of excrement bare-handed, walked over to Herman, and smeared it all over his face.

"That's for the tushy poke you fucking dweeb!"

The Eighties laughed hysterically while Amanda attempted to crawl away on all fours, screaming silently with a look of unimaginable horror on her face.

"Leave 'em. They've had enough for a Friday. I got plans for each one," Debbie sneered as she patted her boys on the ass firmly.

"Ouch," Shades grumbled.

"What's the matter, pussy? That dork's dick really hurt you yesterday? Get fucking real."

"It was a lucky hit, that's all. Still sore, though. Fuck."

"Fuck yeah, fuck yeah," says Fuck Yeah, agreeing with Shades as he rubbed his bandaged yet still disgusting head wound.

"Jesus Christ you two are fucking lame. Get me outta here. Now."

All three jumped back in Shades' ride, laughing and high-fiving over their handiwork. Shades stomped on the gas pedal, and they got the fuck outta dodge before Herman could even wake up.

*****

Halloween happened to fall on a Saturday and as an added bonus, a full moon to boot. Herman was looking forward to wearing his full costume to the party, as it were.

Every year since The Eighties started shaking down pre-teens for their ice cream money, the parties had been held at random, undisclosed locations. They were somewhat of a legend amongst the teens in the town. Sheriff Dutra acted as if they didn't exist. It was easier that way. The exact coordinates were not known until the night of just in case any parents wanted to try to bust it up.

After their most recent encounter with The Eighties, Amanda was back to drooling from the mouth and staring out the window at nothing in particular. Herman tiptoed into his sister's room, hoping not to startle her. The slightest errant noise threatened to send her into violent convulsions followed by urinating on herself.

But it was too late. As Herman sat down next to his sister, he spotted, and smelled, a warm and stench-filled puddle of piss. Herman spoke to Amanda just above a whisper, hoping Uncle Will wouldn't hear.

"Tonight's the night, sis. The end of The Eighties. They're gonna regret the night they crossed the Mastersons."

Amanda's only acknowledgment was a slight grunt. No movement whatsoever. It was enough for Herman. He knew what needed to be done once and for all at the last Halloween party Dutra High would ever take part in.

Uncle Will had indeed overheard Herman talking to Amanda. He walked into Amanda's room with a concerned look on his worn face.

"I know I can't tell you what to do for much longer now, you're about to turn eighteen and way too soon if you ask me."

Herman held stern and confident.

"That may be, but as soon as the moon rises tonight, I will be more than a man."

"What in the heck does that mean?'"

"Don't worry, Unc. Tonight will be the last night for all of this. No more bad times for us. I promise."

"You go to that party tonight and nothing will ever be the same again. Haven't you done enough? Fighting with them in the bathroom? Look where it got you. And your sister. Just leave it alone and get through high school. I'll take care of the trash."

Herman avoided answering by walking past Will and out of Amanda's room. Will sat down next to Amanda.

"Did you put your brother up to this?" Amanda grunted again, this time with just a little more volume. Uncle Will patted her on the leg and shook his head in a troubled manner "That's what I was afraid of. Let's get you cleaned up, huh?"

* * * * *

The sun was in full descent and Herman's senses were getting stronger. His eyesight sharpened, and he felt like he had the strength of three gorillas. Not to mention the smell of a bloodhound in its prime. He walked the streets looking at each house trying to figure out where the party was but kept coming up empty. The night was a bust so far. Herman was afraid he would have to wait until the next full moon. That wouldn't do.

Just as Herman was about to give up, an incredibly strong and distinct smell drifted by his uber-canine nostrils. It was coming right from the high school football field. A pungent, rotten, fishy odor. It reeked like a rotting hellhound's anus. Herman had smelled it before, but where? His memory of that night was still a little foggy, but he was sure that was the connection. The smell led him

79

straight to the bleachers. It was the exact same place where Shades was manhandling Debbie's cooch that night.

Herman got on all fours, vigorously sniffing and licking where the puddle of Debbie dew once was. The scent drifted up his nostrils and soon he had all he needed to crash a secret, exclusive Halloween party.

The moon was just about whole now and fully coming into view. Herman stood straight up and opened his mouth to reveal a full set of fangs protruding through his gums. Next, each fingernail extended from his finger, transforming into razor-sharp claws. The final phase was a full body of brown shaggy hair that covered him from head to toe. All his clothes were torn off in the process. He stood there as a muscled-up feral gladiator beast of the night with grizzly bear-like paws. He looked up at the moon and let out a deep, guttural howl that shattered all of the stadium's Friday night lights.

*****

The inescapable echo of Herman's howling penetrated through the halls of Dutra High and all the way down to the depths of the school basement. Down by the steam pipes, scurrying rats, and discarded old desks was Janitor Johnny. His heavily-scarred and massive frame of muscles flexed as the howl carried on. He decimated a punching bag with a flurry of high-flying kicks and knife hand chops. He even managed to create several large holes in the bag with a vicious spear thrust by way of his three middle fingers to the top of the bag. Just as the howling died down, so did Johnny's assault. The old man collapsed in a pile of sweat.

"Sounds like it's finally time," he said to himself in between sharp breaths.

Inside Johnny's basement lair, there were various weapons of destruction propped up against the battered wall in many places; katana blades, wakizashi blades, and several other centuries-old weapons. Each one had a story to tell, and Johnny knew every single one of them.

A worn-out couch, a single Army cot, and one picture duct taped to the wall were the bare necessities for Johnny. The barely visible photo had a faded date of 1935 on the bottom of it. It was a class picture of a bunch of high school kids Johnny held the picture in his hand as he exhaled with a deep sigh. Being well over a hundred years old made a wizard so very tired.

Oh. About that…

CHAPTER X

1935 was the year a young boy by the name of Johnny Dimwether arrived at his wit's end with high school bully Marty Dutra. It was his second year as a senior at Willington High and a threepeat was on the horizon. He was more than your typical bully. Everyone steered clear of the pint-sized terror. Marty had what one would call today "little man syndrome." No one dared make fun of him due to the fact his family ruled the town with a tyrannical fist. The Dutra name was well known for supplying the entire East coast with beef. They had about one hundred acres of Aberdeen Angus Cattle, grade A stock. Back in those days, just like today, money had all the power. Hell, the Dutras had the school system, police officers, mayor, and sheriff's office paid off years in advance.

Johnny Dimwether did his damnedest to stay out of harm's way, but sometimes your damnedest just isn't good enough. Harm being Marty Dutra and his fondness for younger and weaker boys; an open secret amongst all other Dutras of the time.

Willington High School looked more like a castle than a place of higher education. The halls went on forever and the basement was a haven for Johnny. There were more nights than one could count hairs on top of a head that Johnny sat in the bowels of the basement, way past the steaming pipes, scurrying rats, and discarded books, hoping and praying for some type of salvation. He discovered his soon-to-be lair one particular night when Johnny was just a little quicker than Marty after a savage beating. He managed to kick Marty in the groin, run like hell, and make it all the way down to the basement. There he discovered a whole new world that he was determined to make his own. In between labored breaths, deep in the basement halls, Johnny uttered aloud, "I would sell my soul for one chance to get back at Marty Dutra…"

That chance came soon after. A few weeks later, the school day was at an end, and all the students had cleared out of the premises. Johnny hung back like he always did, hoping he could avoid Marty and his horrendous bullying tactics.

After waiting for hours, more than he usually did, Johnny figured it was probably safe to walk home. His father would beat him fiercely for being this late, but his father would beat him fiercely for any random reason. If it wasn't for lateness, it would be for something else. The sun was going down and he could run fast enough and duck behind trees faster than an alley cat at this point. He had a picked-out route back to his house. A tall and lumbering oak tree provided enough cover with its low-hanging branches and massive trunk. The only problem was that Marty had tracked Herman for several nights to pinpoint where and when he would be at said tree.

Johnny usually stopped at the oak tree to catch his breath. Little did he know, Marty was perched on one of the limbs and before Johnny could run, Marty pounced down on Johnny's back and knocked him unconscious. When Johnny woke, he found himself nude and dangling upside from a low branch on the tree. There were a few houses in the vicinity but just far enough to not hear Johnny's frantic pleas for help.

Marty hung the rope low enough to where Johnny's mouth was right in line with his crotch. Marty Dutra stood there in all his glory with his trousers around his ankles and stiff-as-a-board peter.

"What's wrong with you? Why are you doing this to me?"

Johnny swung back and forth. His arms flailed violently, trying to grab at his bully.

"Because I can," Marty responded in an eerily calm voice as he stroked his cock slowly.

Johnny shut his eyes and squeezed out a grunt of disgust. Marty gut-punched him in the stomach "That'll shut you up!"

Johnny projectile vomited all over Marty's fully staffed member. Chunks of a partially chewed-up ham sandwich, milk, and carrots dripped off the tip of his rock-hard dick.

"Just for that, you're gonna suck it all off! And if you bite down…" Marty pulled out a pocketknife and showed it to Johnny, its blade glistening in the moonlight.

After a long moment of terrified contemplation, Johnny closed his eyes and reluctantly opened his mouth. As Marty's dick slid into Johnny's trembling mouth, the gooey mush filled up his cheeks. The smell and taste of partially digested food and stomach acid was inescapable. Tears streamed off Johnny's upside-down face as Marty buried his cock all the way up to the balls in Johnny's mouth. Marty then clasped his hands around each of Johnny's ears and violently rammed his dick in and out of Johnny's mouth.

"Do you swallow?" Marty asked Johnny then yelled out, "Ride that horsey, John Boy! Weehooo!"

With no warning, Marty blasted a load into Johnny's esophagus and pulled out. Johnny's whole body convulsed in uncontrollable shakes as he gagged on Marty's spunk before drifting into unconsciousness. His limp body swung back and forth, the rope making a thick creaking motion against the branch.

Suddenly scared, the poison out of his system for now, Marty pulled up his britches and hauled ass down the street yelling back at Johnny, "You better not tell my girlfriend about this. I got a kid on the way!"

Mosquitos bit at Johnny's arms and flies landed on his cum-drenched kisser. A dog bounded by, backed up, lifted his leg, and used Johnny's mouth as a toilet.

Spitting, sputtering, and coughing up dog urine, Johnny groggily woke up. All the blood had rushed to his head from hanging there so long. His veins were about to pop at the seams. Someone or something was sitting on the branch above. Everything was a blur, but he was sure of that.

The branch suddenly snapped off completely and crashed to the ground along with Johnny. Now standing before him just past his crusty, dried-up semen eyelids was Ms. Sasha in a long, flowing dark red dress. Her long black hair ended just right above her perfectly curved rear end. A pair of sleek pitch-black stockings disappeared into shiny black high heels.

Sasha kneeled down and gently wiped Johnny's eyes clean with her sweet-smelling saliva, loosened the noose tied around his ankles, wiped the rest of the crud off his face, and sat him upright against the tree.

"You poor dear boy. I think I can help you."

Confused as hell Johnny asked, "How?"

"What do you do in your spare time, Johnny?"

"Uhhhh, read books about wizards, magic, and monsters. Hey, how do you know my—"

"Would you like to be one of those fantastical beings?" Sasha eased her hand down to Johnny's penis and began to massage it.

Johnny blushed before stammering, "I… I guess, m-maybe a w-wizard?"

"And why is that?"

Slowly but surely, Johnny's confidence built and so did the girth in his winky.

"So I can beat up Marty, maybe. Get back at him."

"How about killing Marty. Wouldn't that be so much better?"

Johnny looked down at his meat stick which was sturdier and more solid than the branch he was hanging from just minutes ago.

"What's the catch?"

"First, I ball the Hell out of you if that's okay?" Sasha lifted her dress up and showed Johnny her hairy, juice-drenched pussy.

"Okay, sure. I-I know the rest, I think. I sign a piece of paper; you turn me into a wizard and when I die I go to Hell for an eternity of torture and punishment."

Surprised with Johnny's educational seminar on The Devil themselves, she finally answered with a small bit of disappointment.

"You saved me a speech, sure. But about that first part..." Sasha backed up bare-assed and hovered over Johnny's schlong.

"...I simply must screw the Hell out of you, like I said—"

"Okay, Mrs?" Johnny agreed happily before Sasha could even finish her sentence.

"It's Ms. Sasha, sweetie."

Stray dogs passing by howled at the top of their lungs and a couple of streetlights exploded from the screeching and hellish moans of pleasure as Sasha bounced her firm curvy white ass cheeks off Johnny's balls for the next hour and a half and eventually in every possible position; some made up right there on the spot. Like the Oakland Clothesline. And the Respectful Deacon. For the first time on Earth and even down in Hell, Ms. Sasha was satisfied. Her cunt shot out steamy hot joy juice in every direction as Johnny's dick slid up and down.

Sasha eventually dismounted and gave Johnny the wish he had so generously earned. In fact, she added in her own stipulation to make sure Johnny would never, ever satisfy another woman. He would remain impotent until the day of his death unless Sasha fucked him. At the time, it didn't seem too big of a deal. He just lost his virginity to a woman hotter than anything he could have ever imagined. But, of course, hindsight is 20/20. To make it supremely official, after Johnny has signed the contract in his own blood and semen, Sasha flicked her wrist and Johnny's dick burned off in a painful, scorching fireball that left a small vagina-like slit above his now lonely ball sack. It seemed as if Johnny had to pee sitting down unless Sasha was in the mood from now on.

*****

Being the model juvenile delinquent Marty was, he skipped school the next day to relax and brag to his buddies at the pond where they would often hang out and go fishing. Never in a million years would Marty think that Johnny would ever show up to join him in playing hooky.

Good ol' Marty was too lazy to hold a rod and fish It was much easier to tie a string to his big, ingrown, blood-blistered toenail and wait for fish to take the bait and give his digit a jerk.

Marty chuckled hysterically as he recounted his rendezvous with Johnny.

"You fellas shoulda been there. I had my big ol' pecker stuffed in Johnny's gabber and was ridin' it like he was a humpin' one of pappy's so-called prized heifers! You shoulda seen it!"

Cock gagging a weakling like Johnny wasn't any of the boys' idea of a fun time. Matter of fact, they packed up their fishing gear and soon left in disgust.

"Fine, be that way. Next time it'll be your mouth I lynch-fuck!"

Not giving two shits about what the boys thought about him, Marty leaned back and closed his eyes for a nap as he waited for a fish to pull on his toe. Moments later, the lake began bubbling like a pot of boiling water. Fish jumped out in a frenzy in an attempt to escape the scalding hot water. Searing splashes hit Marty's face and immediately roused him.

"Ow, what in the hell—"

Marty's body locked up stiff as a board. His body sprung to a vertical position. The upper part of his body doubled over backward, his spine snapping in two. His head contorted and twisted counterclockwise to face back in the same direction as his butt. The pain was so intense all he could do was scream in complete silence. He resembled a Bavarian pretzel that got kicked out of the assembly line for being too twisted.

Johnny rose from the depths of the lake and glided across the surface of the water, up onto the shore, and ended up face-to-face with Marty.

"Now you can see how your face resembles your asshole. Right, Marty?" Marty's nose fit snugly right up against Marty's shitter. "Bet it smells like shit, huh?"

Marty mouthed out the words "I'm sorry, Johnny, please don't kill me. I'm going to be a dad."

Shaking his head in disgust, Johnny retorted, "A little late for apologies."

"Then fuck you!" Marty managed to mutter out between painful silent screams.

"How about you fuck yourself, Marty Dutra."

Johnny clapped his hands and rubbed them together vigorously. It was anatomically impossible but who knew exactly how a wizard does what a wizard does. With a series of sickening crunches, Marty's head shrunk a little as his sphincter dilated, anal skin tearing all the while.

"Wait, what are you doing?! Aaahhhhh!"

Marty's voice became screechy and more weaselly as his head shriveled up.

Johnny wiggled, bent, and moved his fingers as if he were a demented puppet master. However his digits moved, so did Marty's body.

Slowly, Marty's shithole encased itself around his noggin and before you knew it, his entire head was up his own ass. One last flick of his wrist and Johnny returned Marty's head to regular size, imploding it inside his contracting lower half.

Marty only screamed for a couple of suffocated seconds before his body twitched and shimmied around a little before it went totally limp. His body lay there on the muddy banks of the lake in a ragged, bloody mess. Fish flopped on the banks of the pond all around what was once Martin Aloysius Dutra. Heir to the Dutra empire. It now seemed like his younger brother Gregory Dutra was about to get a surprise promotion.

Johnny wasn't much for conversation outside of discussing pulp novels and comic books, so the only appropriate comment he could come up with was, "It seems you have put yourself in one really shitty situation, Martin."

And that's how Janitor Johnny became an immortal wizard.

CHAPTER XI

Herman galloped through a dense forest on all fours. The nether-scent of Debbie was getting stronger and stronger. The pure instinct of a wild and feral animal led his way. The supernatural force of a full moon above fueled his anger and determination. Before long, Herman was at the edge of the woods near Dutra Acres.

Not more than a few hundred yards away, a lone two-story colonial house sat. Cream with pine green trim. Every window was aglow with interior lights. The faint sound of thumping music made its way to his pointed wolf ears. There were no other homes around. The Eighties had chosen the perfect spot for the legendary party. No one would ever be able to find it or hear the drunken yells of teenagers and sounds of sex-filled debauchery. In the front yard there was an old minivan and a pick-up truck covered in obnoxious bumper stickers like a barista with too many tattoos. Off to the side were about twenty-five cars and trucks of all makes and models. After a couple more deep sniffs, Herman knew he was at the right place. Maybe Debbie should have practiced a little better personal hygiene.

The Eighties had even done a little of their own decorating. There was a figure propped up against a fencepost near the driveway. There with a sheet over it. Looked like a ghost. There were two holes cut out for the eyes, and at the mouth were the words boo written in red lipstick. A brisk wind blew the sheet up and away. Underneath was the body of middle-aged, paunchy, and clean-shaven Grant Langford, Mrs. Langford's husband. A plastic bag wrapped firmly around his head. Without the sheet, it was clear he'd been tied with thick twine to the fencepost.

Herman bounded up to Mr. Langford's corpse with inhuman speed. The course and dense coat of wolf hair stood up on his back. Fangs protruded through the mouth and his eyes glowed yellow with rage. In one slash, Herman severed the bindings that held Grant up with his razor-sharp claws. Grant's body thudded to the ground. Herman growled low and deep as he looked through a window into the raging party within.

*****

Inside the Langford's living room, teenage boys and girls were all dressed as their favorite 80s characters. Upbeat 80s pop music played loud. Several kids were barely coherent, others were just plain passed out on the floor.

A few more were sitting at the dinner table, snorting lines of cocaine and huffing on crack pipes. A tenth-grade girl vigorously stroked the shaft of some young senior stud sucking on a glass dick, hoping he would share after he took his greedy hit.

The ones that weren't geeked up were making out like it was going out of style. They might as well have called it a mono party instead of a Halloween party. There was boy-on-boy, girl-on-girl, and boy-on-girl action carrying on in every corner of the house. Some of the sex was consensual, the rest of it was decidedly not.

Damian, fresh out of juvie, was on the couch in the living room circling the drain after a hearty 8-ball appetizer chased by a fifth of scotch. On the other end of the couch was Fuck Yeah, dressed up like Roger Murtaugh from Lethal Weapon. Wearing a beige suit that was way too small for him, sporting a large afro, and with black shoe polish smeared all over his dumb mug.

Sitting in the middle of Fuck Yeah and Damian was Debbie's new lackey. Todd. Debbie insisted everyone refer to him as Dewey, though. He was dressed in a large pink vibrator costume made of crushed velvet, equipped with a large French tickler at the waist level. Just like Dewey, Todd was happy just to be invited to the party. He kept nudging Fuck Yeah in the side and asking him, "You think Debbie will pick me next, huh, huh?"

At the top of the stairs appeared Debbie, dressed like Glenn Close in Fatal Attraction. She had on a long white dress, a frizzed-out blonde wig, and was even sporting a little blood on the dress. It looked as if she was pissed and just got into a squabble with a highly irate feline. Or a rabbit? Her arms were covered with scratch marks and bruises.

She walked up behind an extremely drunk and annoying teenage girl in a cheerleader uniform actively cheering and waving her pom poms. "D-E-B-B-I-E is the best, oh yeah! D-E-B—" Before the overly enthused and clueless teeny bopper could finish, Debbie pushed her down the stairs. The unfortunate girl tumbled down the steep flight of stairs end over end. When she reached the bottom, her neck made a deafening CRRACK.

"No unannounced costume changes! Check the group chat next time, biatch!"

Without missing a beat, Debbie manically called out to the overeager vibrator boy.

"I'm not going to be ignored, Dewey!"

Todd gladly jumped to his feet and ran up the stairs with his French tickler jiggling all the way into an adjacent bedroom with Debbie.

If you listened closely, you could hear Todd say drunkenly, "My name is Todd, Mistress Debbie." Followed by a hard slap. And then, "Sorry, my name is Dewey. Sorry, Mistress Debbie."

To complete the Lethal Weapon duo, Shades was dressed up like Martin Riggs, complete with a real 9mm Beretta handgun, bad mullet, blue jeans, letter jacket, and cowboy boots. It was more like Lethal Weapon 2 than the original, but no one seemed to care. He waved his gun at everybody, yelling maniacally "I'm a real fucking cop and this is a real fucking gun!"

He then proceeded to hold the gun to all the hottest chick's faces (and with the greatest asses) demanding sexual favors. "And this is a real fucking dick!" he bellowed while holding his crotch.

Some dumb asshole jock wearing nothing but a ski mask and coke dust was raping some sixteen-year-old girl from behind. The girl screamed and howled in dismay as loud as she could, hoping someone would rescue her.

"Somebody please help me!"

The screams only annoyed Shades. So he aimed his 9mm and BAM, one shot to the back of the head of the coked-out jock. The teen pushed him off her and thanked Shades generously. Still annoyed, this time by her shrill voice, Shades aimed again and shot her dead center between the eyes. Brain matter splattered out in all different directions. The crowd of stoned adolescents didn't seem to care past a few seconds and just kept partying. One of the linebackers on the football team with a coke boner tried to fuck the bullet hole in the girl's forehead while a few others formed a circle jerk around him.

Standing there, Shades blinked his right eye and scratched his head obsessively until it bled, deciding what to do next.

"Dead pussy's better than no pussy. Move over, you fuckers."

In less than a second, Shades pumped away on the girl's lifeless body as brains and cum oozed out of the massive hole that was in her head thanks to Coke Boner. Thirty seconds inside the dead girl's catcher's mitt, he exclaimed, "Godammit, she's not wet!"

Disappointed, Shades stood up, pulled up his pants, and continued on with his best psychotic Riggs impersonation.

*****

Herman's heightened sense of hearing and his flashbacks of his sister being viciously raped were enough to send him into a point-of-no-return rage. He flexed his claws. Saliva dripped from razor-tip fangs. His nostrils bellowed out steam like two exhaust pipes coming off an eighteen-wheeler.

With no regard for his body, Herman smashed through the floor-to-ceiling patio door windows just feet away from the living room couch. The glass exploded into a million pieces causing a deafening sound as it mixed with a roar from deep within him. The glass caused severe lacerations to his body, but they began to heal as quickly as they appeared.

Any ordinary human being in their right mind would be scared shitless to see a werewolf crash through a window. On Halloween. Fuck Yeah and Shades were not in their right mind. Fuck Yeah had his mouth planted firmly around a hose attached to a keg of beer. Shades was working the pump that fed the beer to the already inebriated neanderthal. Neither realized the gravity of the current predicament they were in. All the other teens yelled out "Werewolf!" simultaneously while running for the nearest exit. Only Damian remained with the two Eighties foot soldiers.

For a brief second, Shades was sure it was the greatest costume ever.

"That's gnarly as all get out!" he called out while twitching and shaking his head randomly.

Fuck Yeah started pointing and indicating he knew who it was but couldn't relay the message to Shades.

"Fuck… Fu… Fuck Y-Yeahhhh!"

"Who? The fuck are you babbling about, Detective Murtaugh?"

Herman just stood there while his nostrils flared, breathing heavy from a muscular chest that rose and fell with every ragged, growly breath. Herman scanned the room looking for Debbie. The smell of her rotted-out and heavily traveled putrid vagina permeated throughout the house, making it impossible to discern where exactly she was in there just based on smell.

"Where's Debbie?" Herman said in a gritty baritone.

"Fuck me! Hermy Hair Lip! Son of a bitch, I was sure we taught your ass a lesson. You think some costume is going to scare us?" Shades said as he pointed the 9mm at Herman.

To prove he was the real deal, Herman noticed Damian experimenting with an assortment of drugs. In each arm were track marks from heroin and traces of dried blood. All around him were multicolored pills, Fentanyl, Oxycontin, and various other schedule 1 pharmaceuticals. Damian was maybe a couple of fainting heartbeats away from being dead. Herman could hear it. So he did what any responsible werewolf would do. Herman leapt onto Damian on all fours and bit the junkie's arm completely off at the elbow. It was so swift and vicious that Damian never even noticed the arterial blood spray that soaked into the carpet and walls. The number of drugs had numbed any nerves he once had.

"Just say no to drugs and alcohol," Herman growled at a now paler-than-pale Damian.

To appease his carnal desires and empty stomach, Herman chewed Damian's lower arm down to the bone. Damian stood up searching for the exit door. Blood continued to squirt out of the arm as he drunkenly made it outside and disappeared.

Shades screamed, "You hairy ass motherfucker, I don't what the hell you are but I'm about to empty this gat into your stank asshole!"

A hail of bullets penetrated every body part of his massive wolf frame. As his wounds started to heal slowly this time, Herman chucked Damian's chewed-up arm right at Shades' face. Shades dropped his pistol in a panic and ran for the back door. Herman was now a little faster than Shades, though. He grabbed him mid-stride, spun him around, and sent a massive right fist through Shades' midsection and out through the other side. His hairy fist made a squishy tearing sound like wet paper covered in glue as it obliterated Shades' abdomen and spine. Shades shrieked in agonizing pain as Herman slowly lifted him up several feet in the air. Shades wiggled and jerked his upper body, trying to dislodge himself from Herman's arm. Eventually, Herman lowered his arm with a wolfy grin, and with one push from his foot, Shades slid off and onto the floor. So did a large portion of Shades' intestines. He lay there on the carpet with a gaping hole where his middle parts used to be, choking on a thick gout of his own blood.

"Werewolves…are so…fucking…retarded…"

And those were the last words of Grant "Shades" McGuffin.

Herman turned to Fuck Yeah and pointed at him with a sharp claw. Fuck Yeah figured he was strong enough to tangle with Herman and unleashed an enthusiastic battle cry.

"Ohhhh, fuck yeah, fuck yeah, fuck yeah!"

From across the room, Herman flexed his hairy body. His entire coat was matted with dried blood and bits of Shades' flesh. To add salt to the stomach wound, Herman snatched Shades' glasses off his head and placed them over his own eyes. Cool-ass werewolf achievement unlocked.

Enraged that Shades was now missing his shades, Fuck Yeah charged Herman head-on, screaming all the while. The two collided and rolled around the floor, fists and claws flying and hitting their mark over and over. Fuck Yeah was able to hold his own against the brute force of Herman for a short time, getting in some hard and painful shots to Herman's face and chest. Soon though, Herman got the upper hand and managed to maneuver his head down to Fuck Yeah's upper thigh. His ferocious vice-like jaws clamped down on the brute's massive left leg. Herman snarled and shook his head relentlessly like a rabid rottweiler on Fuck Yeah's lower limb.

With every crushing bite, Herman managed to strip Fuck Yeah's leg all the way from the top of the thigh down to the ankle. Every piece of furniture had blood and tissue on it. Chunks of meat from Fuck Yeah's leg clung to the ceiling fan which was currently spinning at the medium setting.

In a futile attempt with his remaining limbs, Fuck Yeah crawled to the front door. For a brief second, Herman felt sorry for the big idiot. That was quickly erased when his sister flashed a smile in the back of his mind. Amanda's angelic face and bravery in the face of such utter darkness was the motivation he needed to unleash his unbridled wrath on Fuck Yeah.

Fuck Yeah somehow managed to make it to the door while Herman was momentarily distracted. Herman gritted his blood-stained teeth and laughed.

"This is the greatest party ever! Why would you want to leave?"

Fuck Yeah turned his head and looked at Herman with a blank stare. He tried to mutter out a "Fuck yeah," but only his malodorous breath came out in staggered gasps.

Herman stepped over Fuck Yeah, turned the knob, and opened the door. Fuck Yeah crawled out and down the sidewalk. In one quick sweeping motion, Herman grabbed Fuck Yeah's good leg, ripped it off his torso, and threw it across the street. As if that weren't enough, Herman squatted on all fours and jumped straight up into the air about twenty feet. His massive bipedal paw landed right on Fuck Yeah's head. There was a large splat, then mushy grey matter slithered out of his head like hamburger meat through a grinder. All that was left after the stomp was a torso, two arms, a down-to-the-bone left leg, and the bottom half of his jaw.

Herman was still hungry, and his stomach let it be known with a grumble. Only raw meat would satisfy the insatiable appetite of a werewolf. Herman ripped both of Fuck Yeah's arms off and gnawed both down to the bone. Herman's entire mug was matted with thick blood and chunks of skin.

After finishing his bully buffet, he threw both arms into a second-story window just above him. According to the scream coming from the window where the severed arms landed, Herman knew exactly where to go to find Debbie Dutra.

The smell of putrid vagina juices mixed with menstrual blood led him straight back into the house and up the stairs. His trusty werewolf snout finally led the way to where Debbie was; Mr. and Mrs. Langford's bedroom. Herman managed to open the door with one solid punch.

On the other side of the door was a beaten, badly bruised, and badly dead Mrs. Langford. The teacher must have been the feline (rabbit?) Debbie Glenn Close fought with. The bedroom's flat-screen TV was on the floor all busted up, torn down curtains were strewn all about, and all the furniture was broken into pieces.

The once eager giant pink vibrator known as Todd aka Dewey 2.0 was now cowering over in a far corner still in costume. He rambled on and on incoherently about what just transpired.

"Oh my god, oh my god, I thought Mrs. Langford was going to win—" The teen shifted his thought in mid-sentence "An arm, can you believe it two fucking arms, skeleton arms, flew through the window. I just thought those hits of acid were head-fucking me, but it was real—" Now shaking all over, Todd switched thoughts one last time "Shit a mile, you're a werewolf. A real, flesh and blood, uh, terror canine? Aw jeez, don't kill me. I thought I wanted to be an Eighty but after tonight I'll just stay in my room, pop zits, and jerk off! Okay?!"

Herman swiped a claw over Todd's neck signaling him to shut up.

"Just be quiet, I'm not going to kill you, okay?

"Ok, cool—" Todd looked at himself and realized what he was wearing.

"What in the? Why do I look like a vibrator? Do I even like pussy? I'm so confused right now. Uh, can I go now?

"Yes, but first, where's Debbie?"

"Dude, she jumped out the window, tucked, rolled, and tumbled her way to safety! She's agile as fuck! I'll go get her for you!"

Todd, not realizing where he was, jumped out the same window. Instead of tucking and tumbling, he swan dove into the asphalt below, breaking his neck and splitting his face in half.

"Whoops," Herman muttered as he looked out the window.

Herman was pretty sure Debbie, being the nasty bitch she was, wouldn't douche for a while if at all. If she did, he would have to wait for her to menstruate again. Or fuck a lot. The smell was still lingering around in his nose, so he jumped out the same window that Debbie and Todd used. After landing, he stopped by Todd, lifted his leg, and pissed on the French tickler that stuck out of the middle of Todd's vibrator costume. Just like a dog, he had to mark the house as his territory. After that, he took off back through the woods to look for that goddamn motherfucking Debbie Dutra.

PART THREE
THE COCKENSTEIN COMETH

CHAPTER XII

Sheriff Raymond Dutra hauled ass into the driveway of the Langford residence with lights and sirens on full blast. He knew Debbie had been there, but she was nowhere in sight. As a matter of fact, not a single soul was in sight. With deliberate disregard, Dutra did see Todd in his pink vibrator costume and ran right over his head. Brains smeared all over a good portion of the driveway. Part of Todd's head got caught up in the front fender well. Dutra slammed on his brakes, exited his vehicle with the quickness, looked at what was left of Todd, and commented in a calm manner, "Hmm, figured him as a butt plug. Amos Orwell's kid. Oh well, less the EMTs gotta shovel in a body bag."

The sight of Fuck yeah missing his head, both legs, and two arms didn't bother him in the least bit, either. He just stood there, chewing on his toothpick, looking down at the corpse, and then with a curled upper lip, "Goddamn, this was a complete clusterfuck gone sideways to Hell in a flamin' handbasket."

Once Dutra was inside the living room with his hand cannon drawn, all he could do was shake his head. It was a forensic scientist's worst nightmare. Or wet dream. Luckily for Dutra, he had a knack for finding clues no one else could in the worst of worst-case scenarios. It took a while, but he homed in on a clump of long, coarse, brown hair that was caught on a jagged chunk of window glass lodged in the back of the couch. He had no idea who or what the hair belonged to. But he had a hunch the more he sniffed it.

The last place to look for Debbie was upstairs in all the bedrooms. Dutra kicked each door down searching for his angel girl until he made it to the owner's suite. Clues aplenty. Mrs. Langford still dead as a doorknob. Even Raymond could smell that Debbie had been in there. He knew where his own cock seed had been with just a few sniffs. The sight of Mrs. Langford did bring a slight frown to his face and a rather rude thought.

"Shitfire, I was gonna ask her if she wanted to cheat on her husband. What a waste."

There weren't too many things that stirred Raymond's dandruff up, but the thought of his baby girl on the run and scared was too much to bear. It was time for him to skip a couple of Ima Jean's breakfasts and insert himself into the current train wreck that was steaming full speed ahead through his beloved hometown.

"This here's my chance to live up to the Dutra name, by Joseph. Don't worry baby girl, Daddy's a comin'!"

*****

The next day at class, Debbie was nowhere in the vicinity of Herman's keen sense of smell. Nothing. Nada. The school was devoid of her skanky skunk fumes. There was always a slight chance she would show up, but it was highly unlikely. Essentially, there were no more bullies to worry about with her gone and Shades and Fuck Yeah obliterated. The halls were quiet. Peaceful even. It was almost as if the rest of the student body had no idea what to do without The Eighties breathing down their neck. The only immediate problem now was Principal Lipshitz. Debbie's absence meant he would be back to taking pictures of the cheerleading undressing in the locker room and watching videos of the freshmen girls pooping in the bathroom on his crusty office computer full-time.

Soon after giving up the search for Debbie, he passed Lipshitz's secretary Mrs. Madison in the hallway. She was locking up the office and leaving for the day. If anybody knew where Lipshitz was it would have been her. And really, only her. In his newfound confident voice, he asked her, "Seen the principal lately?"

"Yeah, about an hour ago. Walked out of the office with two black eyes and a blank face. I asked him where he was going and all he said was "going to see Ms. Sasha, I've been a bad boy, need to be punished." And that was it. Whatever the hell it meant. So, I said I'm leaving too."

"That's weird," Herman wondered.

"Whatever, kid. I'm out of here. Place gives me the creeps ever since that jezebel arrived."

The bell rang, signaling it was time for the next class to start. Herman's next period was with Ms. Sasha herself.

Once in the classroom, all the students settled into their seats. In the back of the room, Lipshitz was sitting there like a zombie. Herman stared at him, wondering why he was even in there. Most of the students just ignored him. Ms. Sasha whispered Herman's name just loud enough to catch his attention.

"Herman."

Herman snapped his head towards Ms. Sasha. "What?"

"Don't worry about him, he will no longer be a problem. For anyone."

Lipshitz raised his hand and waved it in the air like some annoying punk-ass teenager.

"Excuse me, Mistress Teacher."

"What now, 'Shitz?"

"I need to go to the bathroom, Mistress Teacher."

All the students roared in laughter and taunted Lipshitz.

"Then go, you insignificant little piss ant," Ms. Sasha said with a firm voice.

Lipshitz stood up with a euphoric and almost orgasmic look on his face. A large wet stain slowly appeared on the crotch of his slacks and soon a piss puddle on the floor followed. After finishing, he smiled. "Thank you, ma'am." And then sat back down in his own pee.

Herman admired her orchestration of such ungodly power. The students were astonished and amused. It felt like a new day at Dutra High. That name would have to go now. Plenty of better names for this place now.

It was the end of the school day and all the teenagers had cleared the halls as per usual. Uncle Will had already made his rounds to make sure there were no students hanging around fornicating or doing any drugs. The halls were finally quiet and there was an odd sense of security that emanated throughout the once-perpetually chaotic school. Herman decided to make one last sweep just to make sure Debbie was nowhere around. Maybe Janitor Johnny would know what happened to her. The seemingly innocent yet apparently all-knowing mystical janitor that no one seems to notice hanging about. After searching many empty classrooms and broom closets, Herman found the door to the basement behind the cafeteria. It was a Herculean task to open the thing, but once inside he was sure he was on the right path. After traversing the darkened staircase leading down, a walk through the many corridors and long hallways led Herman into the heart of the basement. It was scary quiet. All the rats had scattered and were holed up in their makeshift nests. Cobwebs filled with flies, moths, roaches, and even spiders decorated the walls, doorframes, and rusty steampipes.

Herman could smell the old man's scent but couldn't quite pinpoint his exact location. His keen werewolf senses shifted into high gear. Herman wasn't looking for a fight more than just a little intel.

It was only when Herman stumbled upon a dimly lit room featuring a basic cot, a couple of milk crates to sit on, a hot plate for cooking, and a sink for washing up did he realize he had found the janitor's true lair. But where was Johnny?

A chokehold from behind caught Herman off guard. Johnny clamped onto Herman's neck with his oak tree-strong right arm. Not even Herman's werewolf strength could loosen his grip.

"Johnny, I'm…not here…to hurt…you. I just—"

Herman was slowly losing consciousness as his eyes rolled up past his eyebrows. Johnny eased the pressure just a little to give Herman a brief breath.

"You made a deal with the Devil didn't you, you dumb little shit?"

"How… How did you know?" Johnny released his arms.

Herman gasped for several seconds, trying to catch his breath.

"I've forgotten more hoo-ha in the past eighty-some-odd years than you can think up in a lifetime."

Herman was confused. He furrowed his brow as he clawed at his neck, jockeying for more air.

"Wait. That would make you like well over a hundred years old. How the heck did that happen?"

Johnny finally released Herman all the way. The kid crawled over to a milk crate and sat on it, huffing for air.

"I made the deal. Just like you."

"Why?"

"Same reason as you. Believe it or not, we are fighting the same cause. The Dutras have bullied me, this school, this town, and everyone in it for a long, long time. Hell after what happened to Marty, they named the damn school after the whole lot of evil bastards."

"Yeah, about that. I was thinking it's time for a name change. The Eighties are done. In case you haven't heard, old man."

"You must be extra strength stupid if you think Debbie and her old man are going to let this slide. You cut off the arms and legs, but you left the head and the ass! Now you're double-humped, son."

"Yeah, I know. But she's on the ropes. I think she's hiding out somewhere. All I have to do is wait until her scent shows up again, and it will, and she's mine."

"Sure, son. Patience is a virtue. I get it."

"Ms. Sasha. Did she, you know, did she…?"

"Best and only piece of tail I ever had but it wasn't worth me spending the next six to seven hundred years here on Earth."

Johnny begrudgingly glanced at his groin area. "And being impotent."

"Huh? What do you mean?"

"I'm a wizard, and wizards live for a very long time. Long enough to see wars, famine, loved ones die, and see young men like you make the same blasted mistakes."

"I know what I'm getting into. You don't know what they really did to us."

"What will happen when the Dutras are all gone and you still need fresh meat to keep you alive?"

Revenge had given him a bad case of tunnel vision. What would he do after The Eighties were gone? A werewolf needed to consume fresh meat, preferably from guilty scumbags, or they would go insane and eat whatever and whoever to survive. The last thing Herman wanted to do was kill innocent people. All of a sudden the burdens of being a hairy changeling outweighed the benefits.

"I don't know, but I don't want to hurt anyone that doesn't deserve it. I know that much. Any tips?"

"Outsmart The Devil, outsmart Sasha. Beat them at their own game. If you can, your bloodlust can be controlled better," Johnny said as he paced about the confines of his den.

Herman was amazed by all the weapons Johnny had collected over the years and wanted to know all about his life. He asked Johnny, "Where did all this stuff come from?"

"Don't worry about that. All you need to know right now is how we're going to defeat evil and restore this town back to a place and time where the Dutra name meant nothing. You kill me and you can free yourself from Satan's firm grasp."

"Wait, what? We? And what do you mean kill you? I can't do that. You're my only friend. How sad is that?"

"I'm tired, old, and can't satisfy no women outside of that harlot from Hell. I'm done and ready to die. Tired of pissing sitting down. I'm a man, damn it."

"Okay sure, but how does me killing you help me?" Herman asked.

"Simple, only a supernatural entity created by hellspawn can kill another supernatural entity created by hellspawn. And in the process, the deal is broken and neither soul goes to Hell. And you get to hang around being a werewolf and whatnot."

"If you help me get rid of Debbie I'll think about killing you. She's one slippery bag of shit."

Johnny walked over to his favorite weapon of choice, his katana sword. He grabbed it off the wall and for the next two minutes showed Herman how efficient he was with it. He sliced, diced, and swung at an imaginary enemy with deadly accuracy and immense power. Once Johnny finishes and a puddle of sweat had gathered at the base of his feet, he looked to Herman with a devilish grin.

"Been training for this very moment for the past sixty years kid."

"If you're a wizard, why do you need all the weapons?"

"They're neat," Johnny replied with a grin.

Herman laughed. "Can't argue with that."

CHAPTER XIII

You can bet your sweet-ass Debbie wasn't dead. As a matter of fact, she was shacked up with Chet, her meathead quarterback boy toy at a filthy-ass, pay-by-night motel called The No-Tell Motel. Located right off Highway 62 on the western outskirts of town, It was infamous in Dutra County for being a wonderland of casual depravity. It was a frequent stop for the sleaziest and worst kind of human this side of Hell. It was nothing to see some two-dollar crack whore blowing a greasy, fatass trucker or see some passed-out junkie lying on the sidewalk in all of their various bodily fluids. Hell, this was where Debbie made a lot of her money outside of the H trade.

The Halloween party from Hell was pretty much the end of The Eighties and Debbie knew it. She had enough common sense to escape that slaughterhouse, knowing she couldn't face Herman by herself. Being Mrs. Langford gave her a run for her money, she had to recuperate from that as well. Everything was different now and Debbie was no longer in control. A reality she couldn't bear to endure for one second more despite her being forced to do just that.

There was a party going on inside room 244. Debbie's current hideout. Countless beer bottles, empty pizza boxes, bottles of all sorts of pills, and used-up tampons littered the floor. Debbie needed to let off a little steam and Chet would have to do for right now. His dick stayed hard for one reason. It was to satisfy Debbie at her beck and call.

Debbie was flowing with the crimson tide, but Chet had no problem checking into the Red Roof Inn. It also didn't matter that he had already blown several loads into Debbie. It all tasted the same to him. There were no moans of pleasure coming from Debbie. This was pretty much just to calm her down.

"What's wrong, babe? My expert cunting-gus skills all the sudden ain't good enough?"

Debbie tightened her thighs up and cupped them around Chet's head.

"The only reason you're down there fishing in my tuna preserve is because Shades and Fuck Yeah can't. Cuz they're fucking dead. So, you better figure out how to vibrate that pleasure plucker and do it right!"

"Okay, okay. Gosh dang, don't blow a gash gasket. It's about time you dumped those two idiots and realized who the real man is. It's me, in case you were wondering, babe."

"Don't you dare talk bad about Shades and Fuck Yeah like that! Now either shove your tongue up my hole and hammer my puss or get the hell outta here got it?!"

Chet did as he was told and for the next three minutes or so Debbie would fart periodically to give him a breath of fresh air as the lunkhead fingered and tongued Debbie's taint holes all around the world. In mid-lick, the lights went off.

"The fuck?" Debbie whined.

Chet stopped and popped his head up between Debbie's wishbone and asked her "You want me to continue, babe?"

"What the fuck do you think, fuckpuppet?"

Chet disappeared back into no man's land.

Soon both of Debbie's legs were vibrating like a jackhammer busting through seven layers of concrete. Chet's tongue was working overtime like a Mexican immigrant in a one-hundred-fifty-degree Fahrenheit carpet factory with no windows. Debbie was enjoying the ride more than she usually did when it came to Chet.

"It's about time your sorry ass uses that tongue for something other than cleaning my shithole after a good dump! The Eighties will rise again! Ahhhh! Ohhhh yeahhhh!"

This went on for another seven-and-a-half minutes and then Debbie was fresh out of hot dog-flavored cum water. The bed sheets were covered in period blood, pole slaw, and saliva. It all mixed together and looked similar to a trough full of hog slop.

Spent (and hungry) Debbie tried to squirm away from Chet but couldn't. Some unseeable force had a hold of her. Chet's head popped up; his face was covered with menstrual blood and he was grinning like a jackass eating briars.

"Your asshole tastes better than your pussy, FYI."

Debbie gritted her teeth, balled up her fists, and pummeled away at Chet's head. The onslaught of vicious rights and lefts did nothing to Chet's goofy mug. Debbie was out of breath and could no longer fight back.

Chet's head and body began to lift slightly off the floor. Behind him at the controls was Sasha. Her hand was jammed into the back of Chet's head. The whole time Debbie's carpet was getting vacuumed, it was Sasha's hand operating his head and mouth.

Shrieks of terror and wails at ungodly decibels emitted from Debbie's mouth. Never had she been this scared. Ms. Sasha continued to act as if Chet was still doing all the talking. Black coffee ground-like blood dripped from his mouth. One of his eyeballs dangled from its socket, still attached by ligaments and tendons. With a goofy smile, puppet Chet asked Debbie "What's a matter babe, I thought you liked it when I ate you out on the rag?"

Debbie screamed, "I need my daddy!"

Sasha was enjoying this all much too much.

"The big bad sheriff is getting jacked off in his cruiser by a meth-crazed hooker named Skittles right now. It'll be a while before Raymond can make this a threesome, you saucy little vixen!"

Debbie's terror was now mixed with a bucket of confusion.

"How the fuck do you know what my daddy is doing?"

"I know everything, honey. I also know that after your mom and dad's divorce, you killed your mother."

Sasha tossed Chet's body up against the flimsy drywall next to the bed. It slid down the wall and ended up on the purple 1970s shag carpet. Debbie thought it was from the 80s, which is why she liked the place initially. A trail of smeared blood, guts, and what was left of Chet's brain blanketed the horrendously stained wallpaper decorated with velvet green limes and baby-shit brown flower arrangements.

There was Sasha standing before Debbie, her fully erect nipples poked through a sexy see-through above-the-ass, hot purple skintight nightgown. She opened her mouth to reveal a full set of smiling shark teeth. The only light in the room was a flickering vacancy light just outside the window. It highlighted the sharp edges of her teeth with a mix of blue and red neons.

Debbie was shaking uncontrollably as she scrambled to put her clothes on. Sasha levitated a few feet above her. Debbie jumped over the bed and made a dash for the door. Sasha got there quicker, landing on her feet, and blocked the exit door. Debbie was in shock and too scared to scream. Sasha grabbed her by the waist, turned her around, and inhaled and exhaled on her face. The demonic seductress's breath smelled of hot ash and burnt flesh and made Debbie gag and retch.

"Calm down Deborah, I'm merely here to help, not hinder."

"W...With w-what?"

"I am a dealmaker and a collector of souls. My powers are usually limited to merely influencing people to perform evil acts. And I can't tie up loose ends when they are of the supernatural type. I need you to place a monkey wrench in the machine. Get rid of an individual that's causing me great distress."

Debbie's curiosity peaked a little more with every word spoken by Sasha.

"…Who?"

"Johnny Dimwether. The Janitor."

"Dimwether? That's so fucking stupid."

Sasha then sat on the bed and gave her a history lesson.

"I'm the reason your faithful but flawed goons were killed by a hound from hell by the name of Herman Masterson. I was also there the night you savagely and mercilessly raped Amanda and Herman and left them for dead."

"I knew that new bitch and her retard brother were behind this. My boys! My sweet, sweet boys. They're gone! And why the fuck do you want to help me?"

"Johnny is the one that found them. Saved them. He's been avoiding me and my… appetites. Above all, he has placed his nose where it does not belong and as I said before, all I can do is merely influence someone to perform an evil deed."

"Okay, so you need me to do your dirty work," Debbie said with a devilish grin. "Soooo, I'm guessing I need to make deal with the devil, right?"

Sasha giggled softly then answered Debbie. "True but you've already given me consent, in a way."

"If you want to eat me out again, I'll say yes."

Sasha cleared her throat, pursed her lips together and dragged her teeth across the top of her tongue as if she was trying to get Debbie's stank out of her mouth "No, I think I am good there. What is it you so truly desire?"

Debbie rolled her eyes. "Whatever, teacher bitch."

"Let me guess, total control over men, right?"

"Cheeuh, like totally!" Debbie gleefully shouted out. "How did you know?"

"Lucky guess."

With the snap of her fingers, Sasha granted her request. Shortly after, Sasha disappeared in a cloud of red smoke. There was a singed circle of carpet where she had been. Debbie gathered herself and walked outside. Before she could get into Shades' Trans Am, some sleazy pimp with green snakeskin loafers, too many gold chains, and a sharp three-piece shark skin suit approached her. Debbie attempted to open the door to her new ride, but the pimp slammed it shut before she could get in. Debbie turned and smiled at Sir Pimp-A-Lot.

"Can I help you?"

Sir Pimp-A-Lot grinned, showing his complete top row of diamond studded and gold teeth. He licked his chapped, crusty lips and addressed Debbie "Listen here you chickenheaded bee-hotch, don't you know I can crack yo fucking lip for reckless eyeballing?" He pointed to his hand with several cubic zirconia rings on each finger.

Debbie continued to stare at him with a fake smile as her patience grew thinner by the minute.

"I suggest you re-direct those peeps to that fucking curb over yonder."

Debbie didn't avert her gaze even a little.

The pimp followed through with a ringed backhand to Debbie's face. Crimson gashes slashed across her cheek from the hard-hitting imitation jewelry.

Debbie pushed the pimp back away from her and stared deeply into his eyes. The mind fuck was about to begin. The sorry excuse for pretty much everything jerked and convulsed for a few seconds, turned around and walked back to his 2019 gold-plated Rolls Royce, reached into his glove compartment, pulled out a pearl-handled .22 pistol, placed it against his head, and hastily pulled the trigger without even looking.

Debbie laughed from across the parking lot and squealed, "Oh damn dude! You missed!"

All the shot managed to do was go through his right cheek and exit just below his left ear. Sir Pimp-A-Lot wandered around his car with blood squirting out of his ear like a garden sprinkler.

Debbie's fit of laughter seemingly broke her concentration and her hold over the bleeding whoremonger.

"Oh you bitch, you done fucked up my ride, my pretty face, and my alligator skin shoes!" Sir Pimp-A-Lot hollered between heavy sobs.

While yelling, he fired his .22 pistol at her, missing Debbie with every shot.

Debbie pointed her finger at Sir Pimp-A-Lot and told him, "Why don't you go for a walk, dollface?"

The pimp went back into a hypnotized trance, turned toward the highway, and strolled blindly into the middle of the semi-busy road, stood there for a moment, then asked Debbie, "What's nex—" SPLAT! An eighteen-wheeler slammed into the international man of leisure's open mouth first. All that remained for the next thirty feet was intestines, chunks of pimp meat, smeared blood, and lots and lots of fake jewelry and shiny teeth.

Debbie walked to the edge of the highway and admired her handiwork

"Huh. A girl could get used to this shit."

CHAPTER XIV

Uncle Will locked up the last of the doors to Dutra High right as magic hour set in. Lipshitz was too much of a cheapskate to fix the parking lot lights so it was ominous and foreboding standing there in the fading twilight. As Will walked to his car, every couple of seconds he would look over his back, to the left, and to the right. So far so good… Until high beams flashed from across the parking lot like two enormous floodlights.

Will was partially blinded and couldn't make out who was coming towards him. All he could hear was quick and heavy-thudding footsteps, keys jangling, and a menacing voice calling out to him.

"Where's my fucking daughter, you pansy-ass sack of shit?!"

"Sheriff? Is that you? The hell is going on?"

"Yeah, motherfucker, and we're about to go for a little ride, so hold on."

Will never saw the bulldozing left hook that connected with his jaw and broke it. After the hit, Dutra grabbed Will by the shirt collar and pulled him across the parking lot all the way toward his police cruiser. Will yelped in pain as his body was dragged on the unforgiving asphalt. By the time they made it to the police cruiser, Will's clothes were shredded, and his body was covered in road rash. Bits of asphalt and gravel had dug into his skin. Where there wasn't road material, there was missing skin down to exposed muscle tissue.

Dutra grabbed a length of rope out of the back of his cruiser, tied Will's arms together, and demanded Will speak.

"Where's my daughter you summabitch?"

Will horse-kicked Raymond right in the nuts. Dutra doubled over in pain as Will jumped up and attempted to run away. Dutra recovered enough to unholster his revolver, aim, and send one hell of a slug into the back of Will's left kneecap. The shot was so powerful, it blew the bottom half of his leg off.

Dutra walked towards Will, the spurs on his boots clinking on the asphalt. Will didn't even try to run this time. Dutra stepped up to Will as the security guard and still relatively new uncle lay on his back laughing hysterically in between every other cough and heavy-handed breath.

Dutra failed to see what was so funny. "Either tell me where my daughter is or I'm going to stop being so nice and end this pow-wow we're having real damn soon."

Heavily breathing and losing a significant amount of blood, Will was ready to talk.

"To be honest with you, I don't have the slightest idea where your skanky cum dumpster whore daughter is. But I do know one thing."

"And what's that, Deputy Dawg?"

"You're a real fucking jerk."

Dutra chuckled, holstered his revolver, hocked up a loogie and spit it right between Will's eyes and laughed.

"Didn't you know it's against the law to lie to a peace officer? Hell, I reckon that's obstruction of justice. Looks like I'm going to have to arrest you, Unc."

"Okay, okay, you got me, Sheriff. I'm going to help you solve this case for you right here and now."

"Finally come around now you's missing a walkin' stick? That it?" Dutra asked with a slightly distasteful grimace while he poked at Will's bloody leg stump with his boot spur.

Will howled in unadulterated agony. "Oh, you son of a bitch! I'll tell you how…" Will then let out a laugh that sounded more like the cough of a dying man. "My nephew's the one who's got Debbie running scared and you're going to have to wait till a full moon to find him because he's a werewolf, by God! And by then it'll be too late because he's gonna find you!"

A dim lightbulb flickered on and off in Dutra's brain. His eyes lit up like a bargain store Christmas window. "Guess that would explain the clump of hair I found in the broken window and the bite marks on that Damian creampuff. He's lucky the paramedics got to him before I could interrogate him properly."

"It took you that long to find out, you dumb, ignorant, inbred horsefucker?"

"Here I've broke your goddamned jaw, drug your sorry ass across a parking lot more than twenty feet, blew your fucking leg off, and you still wanna be a smart ass. Will gosh dang wonders never cease!" Dutra sucked on his teeth for a second while gripping his Smith & Wesson. "I will say one thing though."

Will's face was now pale from blood loss and his breaths were weak and far apart.

"What's…that… D-Dutra?"

"You are one tough summabitch."

Dutra pulled out his Smith and Wesson, placed his finger on the trigger and aims at Will's head.

"No, I'm not tough. I just have a family to take care of."

One shot to the forehead sent Will's brains all over the asphalt and on Dutra's custom boots.

"Fuck me!"

As Dutra looked down at his now ruined eight hundred dollar cowboy boots he muttered, "Guess I'm on the hunt for a flea-bitten mutt. His hide will make a damn good pair of boots, I reckon. Wonder if Santino's Pawn Shop sells them silver bullet doodads. Hmph."

CHAPTER XV

It wasn't that Debbie didn't want to see her daddy per se; she just knew that without Shades and Fuck Yeah backing her up, she needed to stay out of sight until she could have some backup to fight Herman. And so, holed up at the No-Tell Motel, she sucked and fucked every scumbag that came along, looking for just two that could fill the shoes of her dementedly departed dickheads. With the ones that didn't fit the bill (so far all of them) she would overtake their thoughts and convince them to take a walk into oncoming traffic, do a nose dive off the roof of the motel, or just eat themselves to death. She was a real meat and potatoes kind of gal when it came to killing men.

A week had passed since Debbie was gifted with Sasha's deal and the dumpster behind the motel was filled to the brim with the various body parts of unlucky naked men. It was a festering sludge pit of coagulated blood, intestines, skin, brain matter, shit, piss, semen, snot, puke, you name it. Even a bunch of leftover takeout. As well as a few takeout delivery boys. Even the resident sewer rats wouldn't go near the thing. The roaches did, though. Lots of them.

For shits and giggles, Debbie cut the heads off both day and night clerks and placed them in their respective office chairs. "NO VACANCY" was spelled out with severed fingers, toes, and dicks and displayed on the front desk counter.

After a while, there were no more men to interview. They just dried up. The only ones that were hanging around now were random homeless people, insane junkies, a couple twink boys, a few trans gals, and Jurassic-aged wrinkly hookers. All were useless to her. She needed more dumbass swinging dicks. The Eighties would rise again. She was considering Chet until Ms. Sasha put the kibosh on that with authority. Some more faithful lackeys like Shades and Fuck Yeah. She wondered more than once if her powers allowed her to will someone back into existence. All she had to do was concentrate really hard, right?

At the entrance to Debbie's room was Chet. Still. There he was all rigor-mortised, sitting in a cheap white plastic lawn chair. His body was a little past black and blue and showed signs of bloat and decay. Maggots feasted on his mottled dick which oozed an off-white, thick sludge from the rotting tip. The back of his head where Sasha had her hand jammed in was now filled with cigarette butts and chewing gum like any decent motel trash can. There wasn't anything left of Chet to even mess with. Anything decent, that is.

Debbie was catching a little shuteye in room 244 before she went searching for her replacements again. Getting your pussy slammed by dozens of guys and then having to kill them because they just weren't good enough to serve as your unquestioning minions in your retro high school gang was exhausting.

Tootie, the resident panhandling toothless meth head always geeking for an eight-ball, banged and banged on Debbie's door for two solid minutes.

"What the fuuuuck!" Debbie yelled as she stirred from her beauty rest. She opened the door and gagged a little when she saw (and smelled) Tootie. He was not much taller than Debbie and skinnier than a rail imprisoned in Auschwitz. His rancid, rotted gum smile spread wide across his face as he looked Debbie's naked body up and down more than a few times.

"What the fuck do you want junkhead?"

Tootie's perpetually blurred vision prompted an incorrect response. "I'll suck yo dick for a bag."

Debbie looked down at her crotch to make sure Sasha didn't give her something extra. Everything was still intact. Next, she looked over at Chet, still slumped over, and put her hands on her hips.

"I got a freezer bag in here stuffed to the max with heaven dust if you'll suck Chet's dick."

Without hesitation, Tootie dropped to his knees and slobbed on Chet's cream-of-decay knob for all it was worth. Debbie propped her leg up against the door frame and fingered herself as Tootie was having a rigorous fellationship with the expired meatball that used to be Chet.

Once Debbie had popped a solid O, she was done with humiliating someone who didn't care if they were humiliated.

"Enough, dumbass!" Debbie growled. Tootie came up for air and whatever pus that was "coming" out of Chet's dick was now slathered all over Tootie's pockmarked face.

"Where's my—?"

"I lied."

Debbie walked back into her room and slammed the door shut. Tootie just sat there on the doorstep next to Chet. Dumbfounded. Rancid prostate cheese dripped from his crooked mouth. Debbie opened the door again after a few moments and all she had on now was a pair of high heels. Tootie begged yet again for drugs by latching on to Debbie's legs like a toddler but she shook him off and walked down the row of rooms in all her nude glory. She knocked on every door she passed and whistled loud with her thumb and forefinger a few times. One last search for any stray test subjects and then it was off to experiment with her old friends.

"Fresh meat! Come out, come out, wherever you are! Soooey!"

*****

Debbie eventually figured out that Shades and Fuck Yeah's bodies were in a couple of meat lockers down at the Dutra County Morgue. She waited until just around midnight to put her dastardly plan into action.

Breaking into the morgue wasn't that hard to do. Who in their right mind would want to steal body parts? Right minds weren't something Debbie or her goons were ever known for. Even the two-hundred-forty-plus pound, jacked-to-the-gills security guard Rolph Dundgren (currently asleep at the wheel) knew that. Debbie wondered long and hard if he could be any help to her. After all, he was just her type of filet manyum.

After the break-in, which consisted of her simply strolling in the front door, Debbie soon found two fridge slabs labeled with Shades and Fuck Yeah's names. She opened the door to where Shades was first. He stunk to high heaven. There was a large hole where his intestines used to be. The rest of his body seemed intact, but Debbie needed a full body as a base. She closed the door and opened Fuck Yeah's cooler. He was a mangled mess with a missing head. All four limbs were useless. One appendage on Fuck Yeah threatened to prove to be useful. It was his hard dick, its current rigidity second only to fatal priapism.

"Ain't this a bitch and a half! What the hell am I gonna do with just a torso and a rigor-mortysomething dick?!" She yelled at the top of her lungs.

The slumbering security guard finally heard Debbie's frustrated yells and came running into the corpse closet. There he stood at six-foot-six with anaconda-like muscled-up arms and legs that were as big as the base of some tree trunks.

"You got exactly one second to evacuate the premises or I'm going to light you up with 50,000 volts!" Dundgren shouted as he brandished his cattle prod.

Debbie laughed at the big ox. The secret advantage Debbie had over the security guard was the ability to control his mind…if he even had one. In a soothing tone, Debbie commanded the security guard.

"No, you will pull your pants down, shove the taser up your ass and see what your prostate is made of."

In a heavy trance, Rolf Dundgren removed his pants and underwear, bent over, and shoved the taser straight up his own wazoo. Fifty thousand volts tickled that prostate to the point he was smiling a mile wide as smoke billowed out of his ears and his eyes popped out of their sockets like a grotesque cartoon character come to life. Debbie was laughing so hard she could barely breathe as one of his eyeballs rocketed toward a wall and splattered on it like a pus-filled water balloon.

Rolph was now eyeless, lying on the floor with his arm jammed all the way up his own ass and cooking from the inside. A pink-tinged frothy sputum oozed from his rigid mouth. Debbie was amazed at the carnage she just incited. More so than usual.

"Oh. My. God! That was so bodaciously fucking rad!"

One thought led to another. The wheels turned at lightning speed in her warped and demented brain. What if she took the best parts of Fuck Yeah, the best parts of Shades, and the best parts of Rolph and made her very own personal one-man wrecking machine? Fuck trying to bring the gang back together. A fully customized walking dead zombie of destruction sounded so much better!

"Fuck yeah, that's what I'll do!" She shouted with ecstatic glee.

With a little bit of concentration and a level of imagination usually unavailable to her limited mind,

Debbie constructed the ungodly abomination known as Cockenstein. It was by far her greatest achievement to date. She had to saw Shades' head off and then attach all four of Rolph's limbs to Fuck Yeah's body. Oh yeah, she kept the oaf's stiff dead horse cock too. It was way harder than Debbie wanted to work but she managed to sew together all the limbs and connect Shades' head to Fuck Yeah's neck. The creation was a little crude, to put it mildly. Stinking black sludge dripped from almost every seam. The smell emanating from the disproportioned corpse was worse than a dumpster fire full of diapers filled with baby chimp diarrhea. The torso of Fuck Yeah was already bloated, black and blue, and half of Shades' teeth were rotted out. Whatever was going to happen had to be quick because the ramshackle abomination was already physically rejecting the very idea of itself. Debbie had the perfect henchmen now all she had to do was bring it to life. Was her control over all men enough to reanimate a corpse made of three different people? It had to work. She called out to Cockenstein, "I give you the power of life. You will arise and perform the evil deeds I demand of you!"

Fuck Yeah's rock-hard dick suddenly bounced up and down like a springy doorstop. Even made the noise. Next, Shades' head opened its eyes and turned towards Debbie, winked, and asked her, "Where's my sunglasses, Deb?"

All that needed to be reanimated now were the four limbs of Rolph. First, the biceps flexed to the max followed by the whole body soon after. The bulging thighs were more than enough to support Fuck Yeah's frame. Debbie was astonished and amazed beyond belief. Cockenstein walked over to Debbie, smiled through his rotted piano teeth, and asked her, "Wanna jerk me off?"

Debbie didn't want to disappoint her new three-in-one bodyguard, so she rubbed the massive rigor-mortised dick to satisfy his reanimated loins for the moment.

"Uh yeah, sure, but we have some unfinished business to take care of, stud."

Nearby on a coroner's desk were a pair of sunglasses. Debbie spotted them, walked over and grabbed them, and placed them over Cockenstein's eyes Shades' eyes. The head smiled and purred in appreciation a little.

"Let's go on a wolf hunt! Awoooooo!" Then he smiled and a couple of teeth fell out. Debbie thought it was kind of adorable.

She was now ready to rock out with Cockenstein's cock out. The Eighties were back together again along with a new recruit. Just like old times. Meeting with her daddy was still in the back of her mind, but the thought of facing him gave her the butterflies something fierce.

CHAPTER XVI

Herman finally came to the realization that Uncle Will was never coming home. Or breathing again. He tracked his uncle to the school a week ago but only found a blood smear that stank of Will's piss and aftershave. And that was it.

Debbie. The Sheriff. Who knows who else was out there. He was the only one left to take care of Amanda. Provide for her. Keep her safe. She protected him so many times over the years it was the least he could do.

There was no progression on Amanda's status at all. In fact, she had regressed back into a completely catatonic state. Debbie's sneak attack on them in the streets probably ensured his sister would never be ready to mingle with the outside world ever again. Just that alone helped Herman fantasize continually about ripping Debbie Dutra apart slowly and surgically. He stayed by Amanda's side night and day, only leaving to hunt for animals to provide a decent meal nightly for the two of them. The house was so quiet without Uncle Will around. His humming, whistling, nuggets of wisdom. His hugs. His cooking. All of it. A void of sadness and inescapable loneliness was there to stay seemingly forever. Herman tried to get Amanda to watch werewolf movies with her and he would even pitch his ideas for werewolf screenplays to her just before bed. His favorite one to tell was Assassins of the Moon, a story about werewolf ninjas in feudal Japan fighting to break the curse of a vampire samurai and his army of possessed henchmen. He told that one to Amanda several times and even got a few grunts out of her. That's how he knew it was good. One day he was going to write it and try to get it made. A day that seemed so far away with the Dutras still alive and kicking.

A werewolf had an insatiable appetite. The typical cheeseburgers, french fries, and pizza would no longer do. He needed fresh raw meat constantly. And meat to cook for Amanda. It was necessary for a wolf to hunt its prey, kill it, and eat it right there. And hunting could sometimes take a few hours. It was the only time he was truly afraid. Afraid to leave Amanda all alone. But it had to be done. There was no one left to look out for them.

As Herman kissed Amanda on his way out for the hunt, tears streamed from her face as she shook her head adamantly "NO!"

"I have to go, sis. We need to eat. I need to eat. I'll be back soon, just like always."

With surprising quickness, the usually catatonic Amanda leapt off her bed and slid under it, curling up in the fetal position. It startled Herman to the point of him flinching considerably.

After a few unsuccessful moments of Herman trying to cajole Amanda out from under the bed, Herman got on his belly and crawled underneath the bed with her. A sweet kiss on his sister's petrified face seemed to offer Amanda a speck of comfort. Herman knew he could offer no apologies, no swift retribution, or any solace to Amanda. For the next hour, they held each other under the bed, not saying a word. Only Herman's growling stomach breached the silence. He did his best to sneak out without waking Amanda up, who had just fallen asleep to the rhythmic sounds of his stomach. As he got to the door, he heard a voice he was sure he'd never hear from again.

"Wait."

Amanda had crawled out and was sitting up against her bed, shaky hands resting nervously in her lap.

"You're... talking again..."

"Finish what you started, okay? It has to end. For Uncle Will. For me. For yourself. I can't do it. I just can't…"

"You don't have to, sis. That's what I'm here for now. No mask required."

Herman's eyes glowed a flash of yellow, his fingernails sprouted into partial claws, and his fangs protruded about an eighth of an inch out of his mouth. Amanda smiled weakly at him and nodded.

"Good luck out there. Come back soon, okay?"

"I got a new pitch for you," he said with a grin.

"I can't wait to hear it."

"Get some sleep and I'll be back before you know it."

*****

Tonight's hunt had gone on for much longer than he anticipated. Habersham Forest wasn't too far from Uncle Will's house, and it was full of foxes, squirrels, hares, creepy slithering snakes, and other catchable critters. Here was where Herman perfected his hunting skills. He was agile and quick, and honed his skills to deadly accuracy.

He had found a slippery stag that almost got away from him to satisfy his own appetite. The chase dragged and dragged but eventually Herman trapped it in a small cave alcove and went in for the kill. It was a solid meal and would have to do for now. About an hour later he had enough rabbits to make kebabs for Amanda tomorrow. Returning home after midnight, Herman sensed something amiss. The usual blanket of solitude and loneliness felt disturbed. Upturned.

Someone else had just been in the house. He could feel it. A few neighboring dogs were barking intermittently at something that just happened.

Or was still happening.

Upon closer inspection, the front door looked as if it had been kicked in. Herman cautiously worked his way through the living room and up the stairs. Nothing yet. No sounds, no smells. Just blood. And that was always in Herman's nostrils.

Amanda's door was closed. Herman tried to push it open but couldn't budge it. It was stuck. Jammed. He had to kick with the full weight of his lycanthrope body several times to get it open. A chair had been blocking it from the other side, which Herman demolished with his final kick through the door. There was Amanda, lying in her bed with a bed covered in a sheet up to her neck. Her eyes looked straight up to the ceiling. No recognition of Herman or movement due to him breaking through the door. The entire sheet was saturated in blood and the room smelled of copper and urine. The shock prevented Herman from reacting at all yet. He just inched closer to the bed and slowly reached for the sheet, pulling it off in slow motion as his brain struggled to process what he was looking at. Her legs had been ripped from her hip joints and tied to opposite ends of the bed. Both of her arms were splayed and flayed wide open like the flesh of a gutted fish. There was a vertical cut from the elbow, all the way down to her wrists. A broken end of a beer bottle was shoved up her vagina. The other end was jammed up her anus. Her head was severed completely and lay there like a random mannequin head in search of a body. There didn't seem to be any blood left in her body whatsoever. The sheets and mattress were soaked with it and excess drippage collected in a massive pool under her bed. Where they had just sheltered together mere hours ago. The sight of Herman's sister split in half like a wishbone, eviscerated, violated, and decapitated finally caught up with his brain and drove him into an uncontrollable rage. He punched holes through the drywall, jumped up and ripped the ceiling fan out of the wall, and pulled the already broken door off its hinges.

All Herman could do at this point was give his beloved sister a little dignity. Both ropes were untied, legs were brought together, and the bottle was pulled out of her vagina and anus. Herman kissed her on the forehead and draped a clean bedsheet over her once beautiful body. Sadly, he couldn't remember how beautiful she looked that first day of school no matter how hard he tried. All he could see was Debbie's contorted, laughing face.

Amanda's closet was full of t-shirts, a mound of assorted shoes, blue jeans, and several dresses. Only one piece of clothing drew his attention. Amanda's sundress. The one she wore that first day of school in their new life. The one that was supposed to be better than the Hell they had come from. He placed the dress over the sheet and positioned it as if it was on her body.

A note lying on the carpet caught Herman's attention. He snatched it up and sniffed it. Debbie's scent was there. Fainter than ever, but unmistakably hers. He opened the folded piece of paper roughly, nearly tearing it.

It read:

"Hey Fleabag! Looks like I made a deal with the devil, too! This time we made sure to finish the job, unlike you! See you real fucking soon!

Your gal,

D. "

Herman let out an ear-piercing howl that shattered windows and sent the local dogs into a conniption fit. It lasted for at least a long, agonizing sixty seconds. Some nosey neighbors must have called the howl in because Sheriff Dutra rolled up to Herman's house exactly five minutes and thirty seconds later with sirens blazing. No subtlety whatsoever. He was locked, cocked, and ready to rock with his gun already drawn as he popped out of his cruiser. His size fourteen alligator skin boots stomped through the front door loud and proud. Herman bounded down to the living room to meet Dutra head-on. He snarled through his nostrils and showed his fangs as Sheriff Raymond Dutra pointed his revolver right at Herman's chest.

"Where's my uncle? What did you do to him?" Herman growled.

Dutra raised his left boot, pointed to it, and looked at Herman with a chuckle. Several specks of blood and a chunk of grey brain matter decorated the cowboy boot.

"Well, part of him is on my boot, and the rest of him…" Dutra winked and clicked the side of his mouth. "Some's still at work, and some's food for my hogs, I reckon."

"That's a rather interesting story. How 'bout I tell you one, Dutra?"

Dutra placed his revolver back in its holster, looked at his wristwatch, and sighed.

"I guess I gotta couple o' minutes. Always game for a good story, son."

"Oh, this isn't a game. It's for real and it took place right here in this town in 1935. It's quite the sordid tale. Does the name Marty Dutra ring any bells?"

"You know boy, I've heard just about enough of your bullsh—"

Herman pounced on Dutra and grabbed him by the neck, squeezing tight.

"You're going to listen."

Dutra could barely breathe but answered Herman with a low and weak "Okay…"

Herman released his grasp and continued with his story.

"A young boy named Marty Dutra was fond of teenage boys, and one boy especially. His name was Johnny.

Johnny Dimwether. Johnny was unlucky enough to be sexually assaulted several times by Marty. And sexual assault is a tame way of putting it, Sheriff. However, Marty kept his interest in raping boys to himself until one fateful day and bragged to the wrong boys, thinking he was untouchable."

Dutra's face broke out in a deep red as he bellowed, "Why you filthy no good lying son of a bitch. There ain't one Dutra come before me that's a fairy, especially my great grandpappy! He fucked more whores than Ron Jeremy and John Holmes put together before he kicked the bucket. My Daddy and my Grandpappy said so!"

Herman shushed him once more with a firm grip around the neck once more.

"He sucked just as many dicks as you claim he had pussy until poor Johnny took revenge and killed ol' Marty. And it sounds like it was really painful. And humiliating. Doesn't always pay to be a Dutra. Now where's your daughter, Raymond?"

Apparently, Dutra had heard enough about his bisexual great grandfather. Raymond's revolver came out at lightning speed. Before Herman knew it, there was one shot to the chest. The force of the gun was so massive, it sent Herman crashing through a front window and out onto the lawn.

Slightly out of breath, Sheriff Dutra sat down on the couch and rested for a couple of seconds. All those years of smoking unfiltered Camel cigarettes were getting the best of him.

"My grandpappy ain't sucked no peckers! Fuckin' lying ass teeny bopper. As for you, you flea-bitten mutt, guess I'll just dump your sorry ass in the river, and no one will ever miss you. Thank Jesus for discounted silver bullets at your trusty local pawn shop," Dutra sputtered out then got up and walked outside. To his bemusement, Herman was gone.

"God damn high school kids. Ain't a one of them not on drugs these days," Sheriff Dutra opined.

*****

A battle had been lost but not the war. Herman needed to heal and that would take until the next moon. Also, no matter who you are, a shot from the Sheriff's hand cannon would at least make you shit awkward for a couple of days…if you were still alive to make it to the toilet. Herman's chest felt like he had been kicked by fifteen mules and then stomped on by a family of rhinos. He had a hell of a time breathing regularly and vomiting was a regular occurrence for him for hours now.

For the rest of the day, Herman hid out underneath the bleachers at the high school, waiting for his gunshot to the chest to heal. When the school day was over, both the grounds and the parking cleared out and resembled a ghost town of disappointment and indifference. In the near distance, a voice called out from across the parking lot to Herman.

"You keep lying there and feeling sorry for yourself, the Devil is going to sneak up on you and drag you straight to Hell to be his furry footstool."

Johnny was approaching with a bucket in one hand and a trash grabber in the other. The janitor's voice perked Herman up. He stood shakily and took a deep breath, grimacing in pain all the while.

"You're right, old man. You wouldn't happen to know how to extract a silver bullet from a werewolf's chest, would you?"

Herman tried to let out a laugh after that question, but he just broke down into tears and sobs and fell back to the ground, holding himself in agony.

Johnny rushed to him and propped him up against his own frame, holding him around the shoulders tightly.

"I know, kid. I know all about it. You can tell me, now. Go ahead. I'll listen."

"She… I… I can't…"

"Yes, you can. And you will. Now tell me all about it. Tell me all about her."

Herman collapsed completely into Johnny's chest, muffled screams turning into howls.

CHAPTER XVII

Sheriff Dutra finally got up the gumption to send Deputy Elam to check out the No-Tell Motel. He was hoping against hope that his daughter wasn't there but the more days that passed, the more he knew what she might be up to. Once Elam was dispatched out there to investigate a foul smell coming from the dumpster, he realized a dose of reality was about to smack him right upside his head.

Once the deputy arrived, Debbie greeted him with her irresistible and seemingly innocent charm. Elam knew full well who Debbie was, and his first response was to radio into the Sheriff and let him know her 10-20. Thing was, Debbie didn't want Daddy to know what a naughty little vixen she had been as of late.

It was standard procedure for a public safety official to report in every couple of minutes to inform dispatch they were okay. When the deputy failed to report, Sheriff Dutra raced to the parking lot at the rundown and verifiably sleazy establishment. Upon arrival, Dutra jumped out of the cruiser with his revolver ready to exterminate whatever scumbag dared go against him.

He circled around the building once and noticed a pair of tactical boots behind the dumpster. Where the smells were downright offensive. As Dutra approached, he noticed the pair of boots were moving back and forth rapidly in a vertical and wildly uneven pattern. Dutra yelled out, with gun drawn, "All right, Elam this ain't no time to be filly fucking around. Come on out, okay?"

As the Sheriff got closer, he heard loud, guttural grunts courtesy of an indistinguishable voice. "Oh fuck yeah, oh fuck yeah." Followed by guttural moans of pleasure.

Once in full view of the sounds, Dutra was shocked to see his deputy bent over on all fours, trousers down by his ankles and a bullet hole in his left temple. Elam was obviously dead. The shocking part of it was Cockenstein was saddled up with his massive rigor-mortis boner buried deep in said law dog's flimsy ass. Which was tearing in half with every thrust. The grotesque and freakish creation was plowing away on the poor deputy like a jackrabbit on Viagra. All Raymond could do was just stand and watch in slack-jawed awe. He might have laughed a little bit too. A few minutes went by, and dispatch came over the radio.

"Dispatch checking in on ten-one, are you ten-four?"

Debbie came running out of her room calling out, "Daddy, I'm soooo glad to seeee you!"

Before the sheriff could respond to his daughter, he answered dispatch right quick.

"Uhhhhhhhhhh, yeah, you can cancel checks. I guess. Hoo boy."

"Ten-four." Dispatch replied.

Dutra holstered his revolver and asked Debbie, "What in the othergodly creation of hellfire is that…" He paused for a second before finishing. "…Debbie?" He pointed to Cockenstein who was still stretching out the deputy's dead and now rancid asshole.

Debbie pulled the innocent card once again. "I don't know, Daddy. I was kidnapped by a gang—"

Dutra stopped his daughter by placing his hand over her mouth.

"Cut the shit, sugarplum. I knows what you been doing. What you been up to. I'm the Sheriff of Dutra County, and I know everything that goes on here, okay? You ain't fooling no one, 'specially your dear old dad. Hell, you're a Dutra. And the Dutra's ain't always been on the…" Dutra winked his right eye. "…On the right side of the law."

Debbie sighed, shook her head, and threw her hands on her hips in frustration.

"You mean I could've been evil in front of your face this whole time? Why didn't you say anything? Do you know how much stress that woulda saved me in the long run? Christ, Daddy!"

"What I say about that damn blasphemy!"

"Sorry, Daddy."

"I took care a that security guard for ya."

"Thank you, Daddy."

"Mmm. I see you had a chat with Mrs. Langford, yeah?"

"Fuck her! Oh, Daddy, that limp-dicked, hair-lipped nerd killed my boys! The Eighties, Daddy! He killed The Eighties!"

Dutra held his daughter in a tight embrace.

"I know, sugarplum. I know. I shot him real good, but the sumbitch got away. We'll get his ass. You sure fixed his sister but good. Did... D-Did this here fella help ya do that?"

"New bitch got what was coming to her and then some. All that's left is hairboy and the old-ass janitor."

"Janitor? Come again?"

"Johnny. The fucking school janitor. He's a god damned wizard, Daddy. We gotta kill him, too."

"News to me. Why am I always the last to knows about these things, darling?"

Debbie rolled her eyes and spit, annoyed. "I just told you now. When else was I gonna do it? I just found out myself. Jesus. I mean, gosh. Gosh, Daddy. I said gosh."

"Well let's roll then. Is laughing boy over there coming with?"

"Of course he is. I got special plans for him. He's our ringer. But first, I need you for something real quick."

"Anything you want, darling. But we better get a move on soon. Who knows where that mutt will turn up soon."

"Okay. Will you fuck me first?"

Dutra almost fell over backward into a pile of Cockenstein's steaming, rotting flesh gunk.

"I'm sorry. What?" Dutra's left eyebrow perked up.

"Oh Daddy, don't act like I haven't noticed you watching me when I walk away. Remember that day when they found Dewey? I heard every word you said."

Busted, Raymond ducked his head and blushed just a tad.

"Look, I fucked every other dick in this town at this point. Even nerdwolf. Bout time I go for something a little more sophisticated. Mature, even. I know you want to, Daddy."

He shifted his gold Rolex watch to see how much time they had. It was enough. He looked at Debbie, who dropped her rope to the ground, leaving only her open-toed clear high heels on her person. Dutra's pantaloon spelunker stood right at attention immediately.

"I have heard in-cest is the best-cest."

Debbie wiggled her ass on over to the front of Dutra's cruiser in her heels. Once there, she bent over doggy style and waited for him to mount her.

Dutra followed slowly behind her, pulled his pants down, grabbed a canister of pepper spray that was holstered in his belt and sprayed a rather generous amount on his non-government-issued flesh pistol.

Debbie looked over her right shoulder and asked, "What's that for? That shit ain't going inside me!"

Dutra let out a grimaced but pleasurable sigh. "Daddy likes it hot-n-nasty, muffin. You can call my little friend The Riot Squad. Now disperse them lips or I'm authorized to use force if necessary."

"That's weird but whatever. Hop in. We gotta scoot soon."

"I'm weird? Look around Debbie, what's going on over there behind the dumpster and all the shit you've pulled in the last couple of months ain't exactly what one would call normal."

Cockenstein was still holed up deep in Elam's wrinkled, ballooned starfish and hollering something awful.

"Agreed, so are you going to jam that daddy rod up my ass or what?"

Dutra had sexually assaulted many a female suspect in his day, but nothing compared to what he was beating up with his meat baton right now. Once he was inside his daughter's womb wagon, Debbie gyrated and flailed for all she was worth for the next solid two minutes as Raymond hammered away until he was out of breath. He grunted like a warthog as he released his seed into his seed.

"Jumpin' Jehoshaphat. What a coffee break!"

After Dutra pulled out, Debbie turned and with a straight face told him, "I know now why you can't keep a woman."

Dutra's uniform was drenched in flop sweat. He could barely catch his breath but still asked her, "Why's that, sweetie?"

"Cause you're the worst fuck I ever had."

"All right, all right, whatever Ms. Hotty Totty. Let's cut the shit and get this night over with," Dutra replied with irritation all in his voice.

"There's something else I want you to do."

"No. I ain't eatin' your pussy out. A lawman has standards and a code of ethics to go by."

"No, not that. I need you—"

Dutra butted in "Let me guess, you want me to break into the high school with you, get your stash of meth from

Lipshitz's office and give it to…" Dutra pointed over at Cockenstein, who was still having nonconsensual sex with Deputy Elam's poop chute. "…Zombie Horse Dick over there, right? Yeah, I think I can handle that."

Once again, Debbie was shocked that her daddy knew so much.

"If you know so much why didn't you ever try to stop me?"

"I just figured you were sowing some wild oats, cupcake. I sowed about seventy to eighty bags of oats while I was married to your mother. At least." He let out a sarcastic, wheezy laugh.

By now, Cockenstein has assfucked the Elam so much that his stitches were popping out at the seams where his legs were sewn to his torso and decomposed skin has fallen on Elam's back.

Debbie yelled over at the monstrosity, "Hey dumbass, you can stop now. How does some crystal meth for a little pick-me-up sound?"

Cockenstein stopped pumping away and pulled out his bloodied and fecal-matter-covered stiff dick. The deputy's asshole was wider than a can of Chef Boyardee. He fell limp to the floor with a squishy THWOP. The monster walked toward Debbie and the Sheriff with a gaited shuffle.

"Hang tight, big fella. Let me go change into something a little more flexible and we'll go get you some speed."

Cockenstein nodded up and down, agreeing with Debbie. The sheriff just stood there, shaking his head at the giant freak. At everything around him, for that matter.

Debbie disappeared into her room for a couple of minutes then returned wearing a Pat Benatar lookalike 80s full-bodied, purple and black cheetah skintight leotard suit. The outfit covered her arms and stopped at the ankles to reveal her freshly painted purple toenails. Her feet were partially covered by hot pink high-heeled sandals. Her eyelids had sparkly silver and purple dust on them. Lips painted black.

"Lookin' good, babydoll."

"Love is a battlefield, Daddy."

Raymond raised both eyebrows as Debbie did a sexy little dance in front of him. Cockenstein walked toward her, drooling from the mouth while small splotches of decomposing flesh peeled off his legs.

"We better get this boy some pharmaceuticals before he goes and fucks the tailpipe on my cruiser," Raymond said as he scratched his chin.

CHAPTER XVIII

The sun had clocked out and the moon was coming into full view. Soon the night and all the misdeeds it represented would take over for a while. Inside Dutra High, Johnny was running wind sprints in the halls, practicing karate moves on his punching bag, and moving various objects with waning yet still effective wizard magic. Herman roamed the same halls like a feral basketcase, hoping Debbie would show up soon. They were both well aware of the drugs that were currently stashed in Lipshitz's office. It was just a matter of time before she'd come for them, and their trap would be sprung.

The moon reached its height just as Dutra, Debbie, and Cockenstein pulled up in the Sheriff's cruiser. Debbie did her level best to restrain Cockenstein as Dutra looked up at the moon.

"You know what we'll have to do if the Masterson kid is in there, don't you?"

"That's why we're here, Daddy. All we have to do is get the meth, dose up Cockenstein, and let him raise some hell."

Debbie let the Sheriff and Cockenstein go first. Dutra followed the clumsy mutant monster as it moved like molasses toward a window leading into one of the main hallways.

"Son, you're going to stir up my psoriasis and my sciatica if you don't get your big re-animatarded ass through that window right-goddamn-now!"

Cockenstein managed to get his head through the window, but his broad arms were too massive to make it all the way through. To solve the problem, the Sheriff pulled hard and ripped off his right arm then shoved him back through the window. The thing went right in like Flynn. Next, Dutra entered, swearing all the way, followed by Debbie. Before she made her way in, she looked up at the moon and harrumphed.

"How can you be on that nerd's side? I thought we were sisters!"

*****

The inside of the high school was eerily quiet. Flickering overhead fluorescent lights lit the hallways in a dim and depressing rendition of a rave.

"This way, boys."

Debbie and crew cautiously snuck down the halls and to the principal's office. Inside was a large, locked cabinet containing bagged mounds of methamphetamines and heroin. Fortunately for Debbie, she had a booty call key and let herself in nice and quiet like.

The Sheriff stood watch outside the office with Cockenstein. Maggots and greenish coffee ground-like substances oozed out of the stump that previously had an arm attached to it. The stench was unbearable. Raymond had to hold his nose as he told Debbie, "Could you please finish up in there before I lose my urge to eat. Maggots is crawlin' around everywhere out here on my best pair o' boots."

Cockenstein rocked back and forth with a why the fuck am I here and what am I doing look on his face.

Debbie returned with a duffel bag full of meth. She unzipped the bag and showed it to Cockenstein, who giggled and vibrated with excitement, clapping his hands like an excited child.

"Where's the H?" Dutra asked.

"You got a death wish, Daddy? That's like mixing bleach and ammonia. Who knows what the fuck that'll do.

We're trying to kill a stray dog and an old fart, not destroy the whole fucking town."

"Point taken, sugarplum. Next time."

Cockenstein's bloodshot, piss-filled eyes grew wide as a handful of amphetamines was shoved into his mouth. It took about a minute or so for the meth to take effect as the brute chowed down on it like it was Pop Rocks. Cockenstein punched a hole the size of a basketball in a nearby student's locker. Solid steel that. He then walked over to where a trophy case stood, knocked it over one-handed, and to finish his display of power punched another hole in the old brick school wall.

"I'll be damned, I guess his dumb ass might be useful after all," Dutra commented while scratching a red splotch of dry skin on his arm that resembled psoriasis.

"They probably heard that. Get ready for showtime, my men!" Debbie hissed with anticipation.

*****

The crash of the trophy case was heard all the way down in the bowels of the school. Steampipes and air ducts proved to be wonderful conductors of sound. Both Johnny and Herman knew it was time. The moon was high, and Herman felt fully wolf again after Johnny successfully removed Dutra's bullet from the kid's chest. Once in full werewolf mode, he tore through the pipes and bounded over broken-down and discarded desks and chairs. Anything that was in his way got a swipe from either his arms or legs and was instantaneously smashed.

Johnny stood at the foot of the stairs leading up from the basement wearing camouflage army pants, combat boots, and nunchakus holstered in his belt, just in case. His face was decorated in war paint from a time long gone by and resembled a war-torn gladiator. This was the last hoorah for the ol' janitor. Eighty-plus years of martial training, tantric retention, and agonizing waiting had come down to this final moment.

The door to the basement smashed open, flew across the hall, and hit a brick wall with maximum impact. There was Herman foaming at the mouth. Saliva dripped from his fangs as they glistened from a glowing moon that shone through a side window. Herman looked over at Johnny with vigor and a curious grin.

"Are we ready, old man?"

Johnny nodded solemnly, fingering the katana blade sheathed on his back.

Herman's head moved up, down, and side-to-side as he sniffed the air. The smell of Debbie's nether regions was especially pungent tonight now that they were all on the same floor. It wouldn't take long to track her down. He led the way as Johnny followed close behind with sword now drawn and on constant guard. Herman was the bloodthirsty hound seeking out the prey and the janitor was the noble and wise old hunter wizard. Huntzard.

The smell led them to one place.

"Cafeteria," Herman growled to Johnny.

*****

In said lunchroom, Raymond was practicing his quick draw with his hand cannon while Debbie kept feeding meth flakes down Cockenstein's throat and jerking his rigor-mortised cock, working him like some kind of horrific wind-up attack monkey.

Raymond guffawed at Debbie's improvised tug-and-jerk and casually asked her, "Hey sweetheart, you ever heard the one about the two guys standing there watching a dog licking himself?"

Debbie just had a clueless look while she continued to tug away. "Huh?"

"Yeah, the one guy looks at the other guy and tells him, "I wish I could do that." The other guy responds, "why don't you try petting him first.""

The dreadful-smelling cock shot out a brown, spoiled sputum that was presumably cum at one time. Debbie flung the ooze off her hand and told Raymond, "Just did."

Cockenstein's eyes rolled in the back of his head while mumbling out, "Oh fuck yeah, fuck yeah." At least that's what it sounded like. Muscles rumbled beneath the deteriorating skin. There were exposed places on his body that revealed blood vessels and arteries. The pressure from the meth was so intense, slimy Jell-O-like blood and mushy tissue began spurting out of both ears. Parts of his skull were starting to show, and clumps of hair were falling out. The meth had done considerable damage to the already rotting corpse in a frighteningly short amount of time.

No sooner than Debbie had gotten her hands spunk free, a gruff and grumbling voice rang out within the cafeteria.

"I'm here to avenge my family and cleanse this school of your evil deeds, Deborah Dutra! Awooooooooooooo!"

The hairs on Herman's back stood straight up, his hackles going wild. Laser rays darted from Johnny's eyes and exploded a stand-up fridge full of milk and juices. Gouts of lunch liquid sloshed on the floor and bits of empty cartons stuck to the cafeteria walls.

"That fucker's got laser eyes?" Dutra asked Debbie while doing a major double take.

"Sasha said he was a wizard. What do you want me to do? Give you a rule book on the son of a bitch?"

"Time to exert some animal control up in here!"

Dutra ducked behind an overturned table and used it as a shield. He loaded a silver bullet into his revolver and snapped the chamber back, aimed it at Herman's head, and fired.

Herman was a little quicker than the 1,975 feet per second bullet that generated energy over 3,030 foot pounds of force. As a matter of fact, he caught it between his two front teeth, and spit it out into Johnny's hand. Johnny threw it back at Dutra at the same speed. Destination: Dutra's head. The bullet went straight thru the table and barely missed Dutra's head by half an inch. The force of the bullet's gust left a red streak of torn flesh right by the Sheriff's left eye.

At this point, Dutra was out of ideas and silver bullets. It was time to put his escape plan into action. The Sheriff hauled ass from his hiding spot to a nearby doorway and down the hall.

"I got him, kid," Johnny whisper-grunted at Herman. He took off after Dutra with speed unseen from him in a long, long time.

"Daddy? Daddy, where are you going?!"

"Looks like it's a threesome now," Herman said with a slight chuckle in his voice.

*****

Dutra managed to find the science lab several doors down from the cafeteria and Johnny followed him in. Once inside the lab room Dutra emerged from behind a desk and fired every last shot of "normal" ammunition at Johnny. His wizard hunter reflexes proved be a fraction of a second faster than all of the remaining five shots. Dutra was perplexed to say the least.

"What in all Hell's creation are you? I mean really?"

"I'm just the janitor come to sweep away the Dutras once and for all."

"A janitor wizard, huh? Sounds gay if you ask me." Dutra pointed and yelled.

Johnny pointed his finger and flames shot out of the tip like a mini flame thrower.

"I didn't. Raymond."

Dutra managed to crawl out of the room and down the hall. Johnny retracted his flame and chased after Dutra once more.

Just like the showdown at the O.K. Corral, Dutra stood at one end of the hall. Johnny the other. This was it. Yeah, Johnny could have zapped Dutra into oblivion but that was too easy. And Dutra was known to climb over four good pussies to get a chance to fight one bad man.

Dutra tore off a swinging locker door with his boots and his fists to use as a shield. Johnny reached for his nunchakus, but they must have fallen out in all the commotion. All he had was his arms. And they were registered deadly weapons in their own right.

Just as the two were about to lock horns, Dutra swung the steel door and connected with a hellacious wallop. To Johnny, the smack was nothing more than a gnat landing on his ironclad-like mug.

"Is that all you got, lawman?"

Dutra took two steps back in a stumble. Johnny lifted him up about three inches off the floor by his neck with one arm. The Sheriff managed to pull out his Gerber utility knife and gouge Johnny in the arm until it poked at bone. Dutra dropped to the floor on his back and laughed hysterically as Johnny held his arm in pain. He followed up with a mule kick right to Johnny's crotch.

"Wrong move. I pee sitting down, Sheriff."

Without even a grunt or a slight whimper, Johnny waved his left hand in a circular motion. Dutra floated effortlessly to the ceiling. With his right hand, Johnny gently nudged Dutra's leg. The deceptively light touch flung Dutra down the hall about thirty feet and slammed him into a brick wall.

*****

Debbie screamed out in trembling fear, "Where's my daddy?! I want my daddy!"

Herman snickered and inched closer and closer to the frightened girl. In a last-ditch effort, Debbie ripped open the last several bags of speed, shoved them down Cockenstein's mouth, and hoped for the worst. As the meth took effect, one of Cockenstein's eyeballs busted through the left lens of his sunglasses and rocketed across the cafeteria, splattering all over a brick wall. Herman was now picking up speed as he barreled towards Debbie, swatting away cafeteria tables, chairs, and trashcans Cockenstein threw his way. Soon out of things to throw, Cockenstein stood his ground, flexing, gritting rotted teeth, and stomping feet as Herman lumbered forward at full speed. Debbie hoped like hell her mind control over Cockenstein was enough to sustain the brute force of Herman. A nearby broom provided Herman with a temporary but effective weapon. He broke the bristly end off with his vice jaws, spit out the splinters, and shoved the broken end right into Cockenstein's mid-section. It had little to no effect. Cockenstein yanked the broom handle out and connected with the strength of a wrecking ball to Herman's jaw. As Herman tried to clear the cobwebs, Cockenstein laid a devastating front kick to his gut. The kick sent him sailing and crashing into a cafeteria table twenty feet away. Debbie cheered on her freakish creation with renewed confidence.

"That was bodaciously awesome, Cockie! Now finish him off!"

The praise from Debbie excited Cockenstein. He turned to Debbie with his rock-hard dick and open arms but forgot about Herman. Herman jumped up and clung to the monster by the neck. Herman choked the abomination and ripped bite-sized chunks out of Cockenstein's back. With each bite, Herman came away with a mouthful of putrid flesh, threatening to make him gag and lose his grip on the abomination. All Cockenstein could manage to do of any immediate effect was tear Herman's left ear off.

By now, the struggle between the two had torn up the entire cafeteria. Cockenstein headbutted Herman so hard that the hideous monster's head cracked open like a melon. Mushy brown brain matter was now all over Herman's hairy face. The brainless torso wandered about the cafeteria until Debbie redirected the oaf to charge at Herman. Not only could she control thought, but she was also able to control the nervous system of Cockenstein. It made her cackle with joy.

Out of strength, breath, and ideas, Herman collapsed to the floor as Cockenstein ran towards him full speed ahead. Herman knew defeating Cockenstein like this would probably result in his own demise. There had to be a better way.

He glanced over at the cackling Debbie.

Only one shot at this.

A loud BANG came from about a hundred yards down the hallway. It was Johnny, with his high-powered sniper rifle. The shot was intended for Debbie, but Cockenstein managed to step in just at the last minute. The bullet from the rifle exploded Cockenstein's mid-section, showering Debbie with goo of all the colors of the rainbow. One more shot separated Cockenstein's torso from his legs. A good portion of green-tinged sputum splattered right in Debbie's eyes. Her vision gone and her concentration broke, she fell to the floor screaming in agonizing, burning pain.

"Or that shot works, too." Herman shouted down to Johnny.

Now, thanks to Johnny, a door of opportunity had opened for Herman to strike. With his brute werewolf strength, Herman super jumped mere inches away from Debbie and uppercutted her into an overturned cafeteria table. A world of pain and a one-way ticket to dream street greeted her immediately. Cockenstein's legs and hard cock fell limp to the floor, pieces of him sloughing off and melting into rancid jelly. Debbie no longer had control over him, and the reanimated amalgamation was revolting against itself.

Johnny ran down the hall at top speed and gave Herman a manly bear hug, but the battle wasn't quite over.

"Sheriff?"

"Bricked."

"Nice work, old man."

"And I saved your ass, too. What the hell were you doing in here with them? Playing footsic?"

"It was two-on-one for me, Johnny. Two-on-one."

Johnny laughed and asked Herman, "What now? Hm?"

Herman's face contorted into a wicked grin that made Johnny laugh even harder.

"Grab those legs and I'll grab Debbie," Herman said.

"You got it, kid."

"And don't forget the dick."

"Roger that," Johnny replied with a grin.

CHAPTER XIX

When Debbie woke up, she was outside on the football field, secured firmly to a goalpost. Her naked body was wrapped from head to toe with a garden hose. The only flesh showing was her firm little ass and hairy, stinky muff. And her head. She had regained consciousness and cried out for her father.

"Where are you, Daddy? Please, I need you!"

"I'm right here, sweetheart!" Raymond called out as he emerged from the opposite end of the football field from the locker room tunnel while reloading his revolver.

"Oh, I knew you would come back for me! I love you! I was lying earlier, you're not the worst fuck I ever had. That was Chet. I swear!" Debbie called out in relief.

"After all is said and done, Daddy Dutra is going to have to lay down some laws and maybe a couple more inches of wrought iron pipe in that ass!"

"Anything you say, Daddy!"

Herman and Johnny stepped out from behind the goalpost pads and struck a ready-for-action pose.

"I'll take care of the sheriff," Johnny told Herman, who nodded firmly.

Cockenstein's legs started to twitch and come alive a little bit, but Debbie was too scared to command the legs to do anything past that. She kept screaming for her dad.

"Help me, Daddy! I can't move those legs and dick!"

Herman grabbed the set of legs to restrain them from whatever they might do, just in case.

"That's what a werewolf punch to the face will do to you," Herman sneered.

"I'm coming, sugarplum!"

Dutra charged at Herman and Johnny, gun-a-blazing all the way. Wicked shots whizzed by Johnny's face. One. Two. Three. Those last three bullets weren't about to have a second chance at Johnny. With a blink of an eye and a firm command, Johnny shot an arm out at a nearby wooden player's bench and intoned, "What once was a mighty oak will now come to life and be my third hand of destruction!"

Before Dutra could fire another shot, the bench came to life. Dutra noticed the bench barrel-assing at him like a locomotive. Not one more bullet was fired. The old wooden bench went straight through Dutra and never stopped until crashing into a concrete wall on the other side of the stadium. Dutra was split into two heaping helpings of flesh, intestine, and bones. His head flew off near where Debbie was secured. As the head landed near her, she hollered in frustration.

"Fuck me! God damn men! Fucking useless all of them! Fucking fuck me!"

This command was fine with Cockenstein's legs and rigor-mortised cock. Her sudden outburst of raw anger was enough to get the lower half of the thing up and about. The legs wiggled away from Herman's mighty grasp and wobbled furiously for Debbie's pussy. The dick right above Cockenstein's legs missed the first couple of times.

"Ha ha, you limp dick motherfucker. You never could find my hole even with instructions!"

Cockenstein's legs wandered back and forth, even tripped over a clump of uprooted sod, and then fell to the ground. Herman walked over, picked up the legs, and walked back to where Debbie was, aiming the cock right at Debbie's nether regions.

"Wait, wait, wait a goddamn sec. We can work this out, can't we? I can reform. I really can!"

Herman kept walking with Cockenstein's legs. They kicked and wiggled and were ready to fuck some raunchy snatch.

"Hey. Hey! I'll admit things got a little out of hand. I was wrong, okay? I admit that. But just think of how me and you can rule this town forever and ever. I mean, a hung-like-hell werewolf and a rock star bitch like me teamed up! Fucking wow, right?!"

Determined and willing, Cockenstein's legs wiggled out and made a beeline straight to Debbie's wriggling asshole. Its aim was spot on and true this time. That slimy, black-and-blue, and almost twelve-inch cock planted itself deep inside her lower intestines. Shit splatted out with each pounding to her ass. Diarrhea chunks scooted out like Cockenstein had just struck oil. A couple of liquified specks of dark brown doodoo plopped on Herman and Johnny.

"That's gross," Johnny mumbled.

"Go, Cockenstein, go!" Herman cheered the half-monster on.

Herman and Johnny looked on with amazement as Debbie destroyed her voice with agonizing shrieks. Soon, her vocal cords were shot and all that was left was a stream of hoarse sounds that caused blood to shoot out of her mouth. Cockenstein fucked her so much that his dick broke off inside of her. The legs of Cockenstein fell to the ground and Debbie's body went completely limp from the trauma.

Something was slowly sliming its way out of Debbie's ass. It was Cockenstein's severed member. Now it resembled an abnormally deformed piece of beef jerky covered with chocolate pudding. Once fully out, it twitched a couple of times then went limp forever. The ugliest beached fish of all time.

Debbie's reign of terror had come full circle. Problem was, she was still breathing. Barely.

"Finish her, Herman Masterson."

As Herman slowly walked up behind her, Debbie regained some consciousness.

"What…are you…doing? Haven't you done enou—"

Herman encircled her entire neck with his jaw, clamped down hard, and bit Debbie's head completely off. Blood spurted up in the air and rained down all around. Debbie Dutra was finally dead, and with her the last of the Dutras of Dutra County. Herman's revenge was complete. And so was Johnny's, by proxy. Herman spit her head out of his mouth; it flew a couple of fee and landed directly in front of her dad's head, face-to-face. It looked as if the two were engaged in an eternal kiss of incest and death.

"Heartwarming," Johnny muttered and elbowed Herman in the ribs.

For the first time in their lives, Johnny and Herman had true peace of mind. Herman remembered what he promised Johnny. It wouldn't be easy, but a promise was a promise. Johnny handed his katana blade to Herman with a steady hand. Herman hesitantly pulled the sword close to his chest and nodded with a sniff. Johnny told him, "You don't need me anymore, Herman. You now have courage, wisdom, and a lot more weapons hidden away in my basement lair. Your basement lair. All you have to do is move my bed. There you will find a trap door that leads down to a corridor. You'll have all you need to defeat the forces of Hell."

"Ms. Sasha? But she's such a hot piece of a—"

"She's just the beginning, kid. Don't let a pretty face get in the way of defeating true evil. She will come for you. They will come for you. And soon. Now do what you promised you would."

A single tear trickled down his cheek and disappeared into the thick coat of Herman's werewolf fur. The sword was brought down swiftly. As it sunk into Johnny's head, he disappeared in a cloud of dust. A gust of wind swept by and carried the wise old janitor wizard's remains with it. A bittersweet smile came over Herman's face as the same wind circled around him and blew his hair in different directions.

Johnny Dimwether was finally at peace. The deal with the Devil and Ms. Sasha had been broken. Her control over him was gone yet he was still a werewolf.

"Well played, old man. Well played."

The moon shone brightly; a familiar sound silenced the night creatures as Herman ran off deep into the night.

"Awooooooooooooooooo!"

EPILOGUE

A few months passed by, and Herman was now living in the basement of J. Dimwether High School. With the Dutra's gone, the town council felt emboldened to enact some new laws and dedicating the school to the facility's beloved janitor seemed appropriate. Neither Ms. Sasha nor principal Lipshitz had been seen since.

If Johnny had taught Herman one thing, it was that the battle may have been won but the war raged on. Soon Ms. Sasha would be making another deal and Herman would have to go up against her. That day would most likely arrive sooner rather than later. And it came for real one late night while Herman was running the same halls that Johnny had done for so many years to stay in shape.

Herman had heard a strange sound coming from his old homeroom. Chittering, creaking, cracking, and giggling. A strange light emanated from within and grew brighter as Herman approached the doorway. Inside was Principal Lipshitz, standing at the front of the classroom scribbling something on the blackboard. He was still wearing the same piss-stained suit he had on the last time Herman saw him.

Ms. Sasha was sitting at a student desk at the back of the class making out with Satan himself. Satan came in the form of a tall, dark, and handsome man with dark red skin, dressed in a three-piece, slick-ass black tuxedo. Two twisting and menacing horns protruded from each side of his forehead. Lucifer was sucking on Sasha's titties and both her legs were wrapped firmly around his waist.

Lipshitz was busy writing: "I'M A PIECE OF SHIT AND I WILL BE AT THE BECK AND CALL OF MY SATANIC MISTRESS AT ALL TIMES." The same sentence had been written at least a hundred times over on the chalkboard.

Herman stepped all the way in, looked at Lipshitz, who was clearly under the spell of Ms. Sasha, and shook his head.

"Excuse me, teach. I have a question about today's assignment," Harold quipped at Ms. Sasha. Satan bit off a bit of Sasha's nipple in disgust, turned to frown at Herman, and then back to chewing on Sasha's nipple like it was a stick chewing gum. Sasha didn't seem to mind one bit.

"Get rid of him, slave." Satan rasped at Ms. Sasha.

"Herman, you remember Damian, right? Damian, Herman."

Herman heard a deep hiss from behind him and spun around. His werewolf senses didn't detect anyone else in the vicinity.

There was Damian with a missing arm, crouched and ready to attack. Fangs bared like a cobra about to strike. A particular kind of fangs, too.

"Really, teach? A vampire? What's next, a mummy?"

"Werewolves can't sense vampires. So, who's the loser now, Hermy?" Sasha laughed.

Herman turned back to face Damian and held his arms out as a sign of a truce.

"Look, I'm so sorry for what happened to you, it wasn't intentional. I got carried away with this handsome beast I've become. Let's join forces and kill these two silly lovers."

Satan was quite amused by Herman's proposal. "I like your spirit, pooch! But it ain't happening."

"Yes, bravo, bravo, Hermy, but the deal has already gone down. Plus, I don't think Damian ever liked you in the first place."

Damian inched closer to Herman, fangs dripping in anticipation of a taste of wolf's blood.

Satan was just there to enjoy the show. They popped Sasha's titty out of their mouth, found a desk, propped their hoofed feet up, and watched on in all their sinister glory.

The newly transformed creature of the night once named Damian leapt onto an unaware Lipshitz, sunk his teeth into his neck, and drained every last bit of blood from him. After Damian finished, he looked at Herman with a blood-smeared face and hate in his eyes.

"Looks like we're in for a long night," he said to the werewolf boy.

Herman ran out the door with a whine and his tail between his legs. Ms. Sasha, Satan, and Damian all laughed at how quickly that ended.

Or did it?

Surprisingly, Herman had returned with Johnny's katana blade draped over his back, a sawed-off shotgun in one hand, a bandolier of shotgun ammo crossed over his bare chest, and a hand grenade in the other paw. The grin on Herman's face indicated he wasn't scared at all but actually quite excited. He growled with bestial vigor and told Damian, "No, I think the night is going to be much shorter than you expected."

Damian shrieked, transformed into a bat, and out the classroom window.

"Looks like we're in for some fun times, little man!" Satan shouted at Herman. And then, POOF. A cloud of red vapor enveloped the room. Smelled like sulfur and rotting flesh. Satan and Ms. Sasha were gone as soon as it dissipated a few moments later. Just like ninjas. From Hell.

"Looking forward to it," Herman growled with excitement.

THE END

ACKNOWLEDGEMENTS

Big thanks to all those 80s revenge/bullied teen movies.

Especially Class of 1984, The New Kids, and Teen Wolf.

Thank you to Nathan Ludwig (and his informative feedback), over the counter cold medicines, and bronchitis to conjure up some of the craziest shit I've ever written in a second draft.

Thanks to Dawn Shea from D&T Publishing for recognizing my talent.

ABOUT THE AUTHOR

Chad Farmer is an award-winning filmmaker and screenwriter at many film festivals and script competitions. He's the lead programmer for the GenreBlast Film Festival and the Nooga Underground Film Festival (NUFF).

Devil Won't Let Me Be is his first published novella.

His first published story was with D&T Publishing and Godless for his Emerge story "Into This World" in early 2023.

His novella Earth Truckers Are Easy will be published in August 2023 by D&T Publishing.

He's currently working on co-authoring a few books with Nathan D. Ludwig.

He lives in Chattanooga, TN with his wife Jessica, their three daughters, their grandson, and a dog named Feisty.

ABOUT THE PUBLISHER

GenreBlast Books is a small press founded by Nathan D. Ludwig and Chad Farmer that is focused on releasing cross-genre fiction with an emphasis on blending action/adventure, sci-fi/fantasy, and horror. Unique voices with a flair for the absurd, transgressive, bizarre, irreverent, or the abstract are always appreciated at GB Books.

You can reach GenreBlast Books on social media via @genreblastbooks. Or you can email them at genreblastbooks@gmail.com

Our website is: https://www.genreblastbooks.com

Please leave a review for this book and other GenreBlast Books releases on Amazon, Goodreads, and anywhere else you are able to do so. It helps authors immensely.

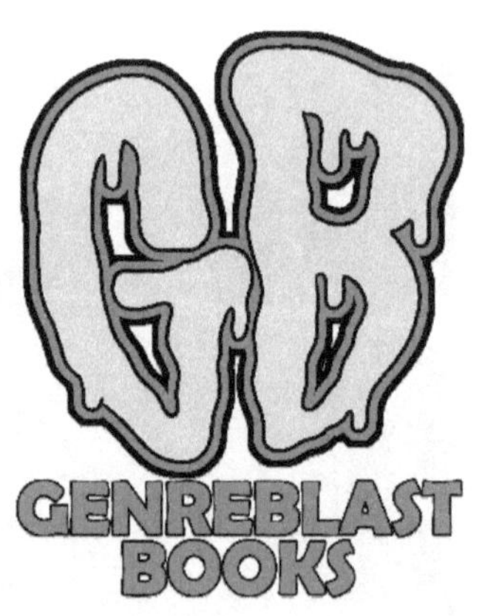